I0788431

GHOSTS FROM THE PAST

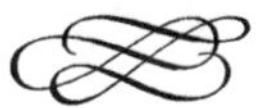

BONNIE ELIZABETH

MY BIG FAT ORANGE CAT PUBLISHING

Ghosts from the Past
My Big Fat Orange Cat
Gothic Novel January 2018

Copyright 20138
Bonnie Elizabeth Koenig

Cover Copyright © Bonnie Koenig
Cover Image Copyright "LarioTus" | Deposit Photo

My Big Fat Orange Cat Publishing
MyBigFatOrangeCat.com

ISBN: 978-0-9980829-4-3 Trade Paperback
ISBN: 978-1-953363-11-4 Large Print

CHAPTER 1

I'm sure there are better ways to fill out a resume and heal after a divorce than running off to the tip of Nova Scotia to work in a possibly haunted Manor set on the coast on the edge of nowhere. This is particularly true, if as a child, one has been told that one is sensitive to ghosts. Not that anyone told me that there might be ghosts at the Manor when I took the job, but all the same, one should always think ghosts when one thinks of an old house. Still, I can only say that at the time I made that decision I wasn't in the clearest frame of mind.

I was at home alone, as always, since my husband of ten years had left me, sitting on our once white sofa, which was now more of an ecru and smelled faintly of his aftershave. The white leather had never been my choice. Kyle, however, had loved it. Still, here it remained in the condo we had purchased together and that he had given up to run off with his boy toy.

It's not that I was upset that he left me for a man. I had always known that he had no particular preference when it came to the sexes. It was that he left me for someone ten years younger than I was just as he neared forty. Plus, all those things he had to have, like the sofa, that I had hated because of their impracticality, remained in the condo with me.

The glass coffee table, a perpetual trap for fingerprints and water splashes, faced the sofa. Also Kyle's idea. Only the sixty-inch flat screen that had once hung over the fireplace had gone with him. In its place I had a humble twenty-four inch thing that didn't quite fill out the space. At least the frame was black to match the black granite that surrounded the gas fireplace.

At thirty-eight, I was a failure. I was a failure as a woman, clearly, because my husband no longer found me attractive. No matter that I might know his equal fondness for men—we'd often shared a few jokes and a bit of leering at good-looking guys in bars—it still made me feel a bit weird that I'd been thrown over for a boy. Or young man. Or whatever you wanted to call him.

Then, as I'd begun to throw myself into my

work at the library, I'd been passed over for a promotion I had thought I was a shoe-in for. Instead, I learned late in the game that they'd decided to look outside the library structure and hire someone new. Bring in new blood and new faces.

So, on the fateful night that I learned about the job set in Schilling Manor, I was sitting in the silence of the room. I was a thirty-eight-year-old woman with a television that didn't match the dimensions of her living room, alone with too many fancy bottles of wine sitting empty around on the kitchen counter, and a half-full one on the coffee table.

Tessie arrived that night with news that would change my life. She was my best friend since preschool. If we were younger, we'd say "BFF," but as a librarian, I hate that sort of abuse of language. I think such things should be spelled out. Tessie laughs at me.

"You can't stop time, Lara," she'd say.

She arrived to the sound of a key in the lock. For a moment I thought of Kyle, but quickly remembered it couldn't be him.

Tessie flounced in, dressed up as if she were going dancing instead of coming here. She'd asked for a key when Kyle had moved out. I'd given it to her. I knew why she wanted it, and later on, she confirmed it. She'd wanted it in case I stopped answering the door and her phone calls.

She was afraid of what I might do. The ease of which I'd given away a key suggested I was, too.

"Another bottle of wine?" Tessie asked. It wasn't a judgement, just a question. Her flirty red dress flapped around her long legs as she took in the room. Her long brown hair, which normally curled, had been ironed flat and colored to a deep auburn that looked beautiful with her hazel eyes.

"Only one," I said. As it had been each night. I'm not normally much of a drinker. Another change for me.

"If you're going to wallow, you ought to at least put on music," Tessie said. She flopped down, her dress hitching so that I got a look at her bare thighs.

I shrugged. "Aren't you going dancing?" I wasn't dressed for it. I was in sweats that had needed washing last Thursday, but I was too depressed to take on the task. I barely kept my work clothing clean.

I still went to work even without the promotion. I had to pay the bills, which my salary did—just. Kyle had been the real breadwinner and he'd been kind when he'd signed over the condo to me alone. He probably even thought he was being kind leaving me with the furniture I hated.

"I am, later," Tessie said. "But I saw something online that you have to see."

"Why?"

"It's the perfect job. It will get you out of here. Out of these memories. You can rent the condo out for a bit more money to put aside and you'll get a good salary there. You are perfect for it!"

I raised an eyebrow.

Tessie smiled. She knew I'd sort of hunted around for a job. But it had been a half-hearted look at Indeed and Glassdoor without ever putting in a resume. More of a hope or a wish. It was all I had the energy for at that time.

She pulled up her phone with its rhinestone case and set it in front of my face. She leaned closer and her perfume drowned out the smell of Kyle's aftershave.

"Look. 'Seeking research librarian. Must understand valuation of old books...'" Tessie read through the description even as she forced me to see it on her phone. Perhaps she was worried I had had so much wine that I couldn't focus.

I had to admit, as she listed the criteria, she was right. I was perfect for it. The downside, to me, was that it was in Cape Breton, which my wine-fogged South Carolina mind had to spend a few moments parsing before I realized that was the northern part of Nova Scotia.

"I'm not a Canadian citizen," I said.

"No excuses," Tessie said. "I bet, considering this is a U.S. website, that they're willing to work with you on the work permits. It's a one-year job and the pay is twice what you get now. Plus you're doing a variety of things that will look great on your resume. And the change of venue will be good for you."

"You trying to get rid of me?" I mumbled, feeling near tears.

Tessie hugged me. "Oh, no. I'm trying to get you back."

In later days, Tessie would wonder how I had survived my ghostly and non-ghostly encounters to come back to her at all. I suspected she thought perhaps she should have let me heal in my own time.

CHAPTER 2

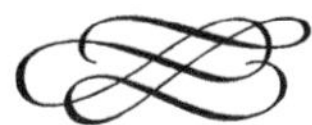

Six and a half months later, as the days lengthened into summer, I rounded the last bend and got my first look at Schilling Manor. My clothes felt lived in after six days on the road, stopping only at night to sleep and shower. I had changed the clothing, but after a long day in the car, I felt like the stale French fries my Honda smelled of.

I'd spent so much time in the car listening to my usual music selections that I'd gotten bored with them and had turned on classical. As the sun was setting behind low gray clouds that signaled rain was coming, the radio blasted Rachmaninoff's "Prelude in G Minor." It reflected the mood of the Manor.

Sydney, Nova Scotia, a small port town known for its famous fiddle which sits on the wharf greeting cruise ships, was the nearest town to Schilling Manor. I could stock up on food there but I'd shopped earlier when I'd noticed that Sydney would take me a few miles out of my way and I just wanted to stop driving. I had easy-to-eat snacks as meals were provided.

"Bethany wants us to provide meals as the kitchen is kind of an electrical hazard," Nathan told me.

Nathan was the boss, overseeing the full valuation of everything on the estate. It was a long process involving me, an antiques dealer, and an art expert of some sort. The Manor was full of stuff that needed evaluation and cataloging. Other experts had done the valuation for the estate taxes, but Bethany wanted further information on everything there, specific information on each item her aunt had left her so she could more easily determine whether she sold, donated, or kept them.

They'd determined that cataloging the books and sorting them would take six months to a year, which suggested the collection was rather large. I'd seen pictures of the main library and was told there were a few boxes in the upstairs schoolroom as well as a smaller personal collection.

I'd hesitated about the job at first. After all, a

job for six months or a year was fine, but then what? Fortunately, I had enough seniority at the university to request a sabbatical. At my staff level I was eligible just like a faculty member. That allowed me to jump at the chance to go. I'm sure my coworkers were thrilled to see the back of me given that I'd hardly been myself since Kyle had left me.

There was a whirlwind of work permits, storing my possessions in Tessie's basement, and finding a good broker to manage to my condo in South Carolina. My parents, who lived just outside of Pittsburg, were perplexed by my choice to live in Nova Scotia for nearly a year.

"It gets cold up there," my mother said. As if this was news. "Do you even have a winter coat anymore? You were horribly under dressed when you came home last Christmas."

"I'm sure I can purchase one there. It's not like I'll need it right away," I said. And anything I purchased in Sydney was likely to be a darn sight warmer than what I could buy in Columbia, where I lived. After all, who needs a winter coat in South Carolina? A rain jacket maybe.

"That's your Pittsburg blood showing," Tessie laughed.

We'd both gone to Clemson to escape the cold winters and had stayed in town after graduation.

I'd gone to Chapel Hill, a few hours north, to get my masters in library science but then I'd come back and found work at a college nearby. Tessie had immediately found work in South Carolina's government, despite her rather liberal leanings. It had been a joy to know that she and I would be living in the same city.

We had lived for weekends away in Myrtle Beach and Beaufort. Even when I was married to Kyle, we'd had girls' weekends away. Now, I often wondered what he was doing during those same weekends.

I knew I could handle cold even if I didn't love it the way I loved the sun and, secretly, even the humidity.

Now I was leaving that.

Because of Kyle.

Sitting in my car, smelling of old food, looking at the Manor, its old red brick and thick white mortar that looked half crumbled, made me long for the perfectly kept historical relics in Charleston. This was anything but perfectly kept. In fact, I worried that it would fall down around me if I sneezed when I went to bed.

The trees lining the drive that curved inward were bare of leaves, despite it going into summer. Their skeletal arms reached out to grab at visitors, but only half-heartedly as there didn't even seem to be enough life in them to be properly frightening.

The gray light made everything about the manor seem sad. It was easy to imagine a woman on the widow's walk that sat on the highest portion of the roof. She'd have looked out behind me as waves crashed against the shore, wondering if her husband had come home from the sea.

The road had been just far enough inland so I hadn't seen those waves, but I could imagine them. I carefully followed the drive, which was mostly gravel with weeds sticking up through the rock here and there. How long had it been since anyone had cared for the place?

I glanced at the place again, noting that the doors were painted white, which seemed to glisten and I wondered if someone had replaced those. How much of the Manor needed to be replaced or repaired? How much had been done? The long, tall windows that let in narrow strips of light inside were covered with drapes that looked gray from this angle, told me nothing. The old brick and cracked concrete that made up the three low steps that led to the white front doors told me little else.

The Manor was three stories, at least, if I was counting correctly. There was an attic as well. The widow's walk came out of a door that appeared directly over the entry, out from what once may have been an attic dormer. The roof was covered in black plastic tarps held down by something I couldn't see. Clearly it was under repair.

It made me wonder about the library. I'd seen pictures but I'd pictured a stately old room with clean wooden shelves filled with antique books that I'd catalog. Now, I worried the pictures I had seen and my imagination had given me the wrong impression. Still, they were books, my passion.

I'd studied antique books and book making. While I loved research, this kind of study was slightly less popular, offering me more job opportunities. The book making was more of a hobby than anything of use, though.

My studies were the reason I worked at a university level library, the assistant to the head of the archives. I knew that had I become head of the archives, it would have meant more political and managerial work rather than the restoration and cataloging I loved, but I had hoped—no, I had expected—that I would get the job and still be able to keep my hand in.

I'd even had to train the new head of archives before leaving on sabbatical. She'd been a little hesitant about the timing of my leaving but this way she could sink or swim on her own.

Looking at the condition of the Manor, I was regretting this. In the archives, books were cared for. If the building wasn't any more cared for than this, what about the books?

I pulled up close to the front of the large building, noting where the window ledges were cracked, the shutters hanging askew, and even a few bricks were looking less than stable. Safety issues, once again, crossed my mind.

A curtain twitched on the second floor.

I drove slowly around the building, following the track. There, I saw that a long wing jutted out the back and it was in slightly better condition than the front, but it still wasn't the sort of place anyone would call move-in ready. There was a large square of weeds and gravel filled with an assortment of cars and trucks.

Behind that was an outbuilding that might have been a carriage house a hundred years ago. That was definitely falling down with gray wood and roof tiles falling in halfway across the building. Weeds sprang up around the outside of the walls.

I parked next to one of the other cars, a gray SUV. This one was from Quebec. Not quite so far as I was, I didn't think, at least not in terms of different weather, but still a long way to travel. I wondered which one of the workers it was.

I climbed out of my car and started across the gravel. Rain began to splatter lightly. It was more of a mist and it didn't seem in any hurry to fall harder. There was a sort of portico on this side, with a raised ramp going up to an enormous door with ten small panels.

As I got closer, I saw that the panels were carved images of leaves and flowers. It was beautifully done, if a bit faded. I looked for a bell. The brick here was red and black and even some white. There were splatters of mortar as if someone had done a sloppy job of repairing and some of that was darkened with time.

I finally spotted a bell, almost hidden in all the clutter of splatters and brickwork. I pressed it, wondering how they'd fastened it and if there was electricity to run it.

I seemed to recall Nathan telling me that while internet service could be spotty and the man who ran the cable was practically living there trying to keep it more on than off, they did have electricity. He'd said it with an excitement I hadn't understood until just this moment.

There were empty sconces above the bell, rusted metal that had once probably held candles. I suddenly realized that Bethany's fears about the kitchens were probably because whatever wiring had been done had no doubt been done long after the house was built.

I swallowed as I waited. Thunder sounded, echoing around me. I nearly jumped.

The door creaked open and a woman stood there.

"Yes?" she said.

"I'm Lara Rochester. I'm here to sort through the library?" I said.

"Lara!" she said. "I'm glad you made it. They're saying the storm coming in is going to be a bad one."

She practically pulled me in the door as if just by being inside I was safer. The entry here was rather dim but it was almost as formal as I imagined the front to be. It was rather narrow, though. The wall behind her was covered in thick dark paneling. A rather plain light was on the wall behind her but it didn't do much to push back the shadows.

"I have my things packed in the car," I said.

"Give me your keys. I'll have Jimmy bring everything up to your room," she said. "Don't worry. It's part of his job. Nathan will help if need be, and so will I. You've been driving."

I nodded, digging out my keys that had, as always, fallen to the bottom of my purse. I gave them to her.

"I'm Maggie," she said. "Jack of all trades around here and keeping things running for the rest of you. If you have problems, you tell me and I'll try and get someone out to fix it."

She rounded a corner. There was a narrow

stair there, and, of all things, a small yellow and black walkie-talkie. Maggie picked it up and pressed a button.

"Jimmy?" she said. "Lara's here. I'm leaving her keys near the side door. You'll want to bring in her things before the storm starts."

I heard static and a response that sounded like he'd be right down.

"Good then," Maggie said to the walkie-talkie.

Turning to me, Maggie explained. "Bethany wanted to have an intercom system put in but they'd have to pull the walls down to wire it. That will happen in time, of course, but for now, we have those things." She pointed casually. "We've configured them all to be on the same channel. They're just cheap things from an outdoor store but they work here which is more than I can say about a lot of the stuff we've thought about. In theory, we have cell phone coverage, but don't count on it. We almost never have it from the first floor, but you sometimes get it upstairs."

Maggie turned away and started up the stairs before I could respond. My shoulders touched the walls on both sides of the stairs and I noticed that Maggie's shoulders, which were wider than mine, swept off any dust that might have accumulated. I realized why she was wearing jeans and a worn-looking flannel shirt.

She reached the next floor and made a quick

turn to the left. The ascent had been longer than I was used to in my condo, so the ceilings throughout the Manor must be high. Either that or the steps were lower, or perhaps both.

"We're in the new wing," Maggie said. The nearly black paneling that continued to line the walls belied her comment about "new".

I must have looked surprised.

"You don't want to see the main manor yet, not at night. No one really goes to the main part of the house at night. The floors creak, and although we've had workers in there, no one is certain how sound the floors are. The electricity hasn't been updated there but we have plenty of electric lanterns scattered around."

I nodded. None of this had been in the interview.

My room was the fourth door on the right of the hallway. "Your room looks over the old orchard area and the old greenhouse," Maggie said as she opened it. I noticed there was a new lock on the door.

The door itself was black wood, the same as the paneling. It, and all the others, had barely stood out in the hallway. It opened with a slight creak. The room smelled of artificial lavender, and I wondered if that was Maggie's touch to make it less musty, as in the stairwell I had smelled, and even felt, as if I were walking through the pages of an old book.

Inside, there was a new looking bed with a simple headboard, probably a queen size. Still, there was plenty of space around it. Two nightstands and a dresser that looked like they were from IKEA sat around the edges of the room. There was a large boxy thing that I realized must be an old wardrobe.

"We've left the wardrobe, as even this wing didn't have proper closets," Maggie said. "And it's been remodeled to have a simple bath."

She pointed to the door. I looked in there and a surprisingly modern room greeted me with white and dark blue subway tiles. There was a gleaming white pedestal sink and toilet. The tub and shower combo competed across from those two as to which could gleam the brightest in the light, which flickered slightly but was still bright enough to work by.

"We have electricity in this wing," Maggie said. "And it's mostly been redone so it should be safe enough to use whatever you have to. The kitchen is on a different breaker and that hasn't been redone since about 1940, which means only the hired cooks can work in there, although you're allowed to store any food you have in the refrigerator. Just mind that it's small and we all have to use it."

I nodded.

"Any questions?" Maggie asked.

I had plenty of them. I was about to start when a dark shadow passed by behind her. It was not followed by a human walking down the hall. Any thought of what I wanted to ask flew out of my mind.

CHAPTER 3

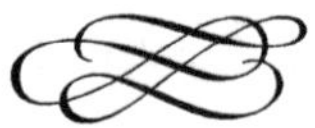

I gaped at Maggie for a few seconds that felt much longer. It seemed like shadows grew around us before she decided to turn around. She clearly noticed nothing.

"It's the lights here. They flicker oddly. Everyone thinks they see a strange shadow walking down the hall," Maggie assured me. She reached in to give me a hug, smelling of freshly baked bread that made my stomach rumble.

I was letting her go and leaning back when I saw another shadow. This one was accompanied by a slight squeak on the boards and then a young man appeared.

"Hey Jimmy," Maggie said turning. "You've come just in time to find that Lara got see one of our famous shadows."

Jimmy held two of my suitcases, one under his arm, my laptop case over his shoulder, and my grocery bags in the other hand. That meant there were two boxes of books and paperwork that I wanted on hand and one more small suitcase, more of a makeup case, really.

"I should go down with you and get the last of it," I said.

Jimmy waved me off. "I've got this. I spent the last couple of months hauling and building with the contractors in here. This is nothing." He gave me a quick smile that was clearly genuine.

Maggie nodded at me, pushing me further into the room. She pointed to the one nightstand where I saw a yellow and black walkie-talkie. "That's yours. Carry it with you wherever you go. The house can be confusing, especially at first."

"Sometimes even past the first," Jimmy added, as he carefully set my things down near the dresser. He waved as he left. His slightly too long blonde hair moved in rhythm with his walk. He acted very mature but looked very young, which made me wonder how old he was.

"Jimmy would know," Maggie said. She turned to move my computer out of the pile and set it beside the bed. She pointed to a power strip there. "You'll want to use the surge protector for this. Lots of odd things with the electricity. Nathan has his computer at the shop in Sydney trying to recover files after he had his plugged directly into the wall. He's just across the hall, by the way."

I wasn't sure what to make of that information. Did Maggie expect we'd be having trysts in the middle of the night?

"But Jimmy…" Maggie shook her head as her voice trailed off. She opened a curtain. Outside the window, evening was blue gray and darkening. There were splatters of water against the pane. I didn't feel a draft, so I could only figure that new windows had been added. "Jimmy gets lost at least once a week even though he's probably been here longer than any of us."

"Even you?" I asked. Maggie seemed so completely confident being charge that I would have thought she'd been there for years.

"Oh, yes. Jimmy used to work for Ms. Schilling. Out in the garden, such as it was. Of course, towards the end, she refused to let him do anything, which is why nearly everything is dead."

I nodded. "The upkeep on a place like this must get expensive."

"I sometimes think it costs more to keep up this place than the entire Canadian government." Maggie laughed. "But at least I don't have to pay for this!"

I wondered where the money was coming from for all the renovations as I looked outside.

There was a broken down greenhouse but I also saw some new glass panes as if they were repairing it. Surely if the place was going to be sold, that would be a place to cut corners. Did you really need a greenhouse that ran the length of a Manor of this size?

"It's not that Ms. Schilling didn't have the money. She had more than she knew what to do with, but she was always certain that someone was trying to rob her," Maggie said. "Poor Jimmy did what he could and there are a couple of the old trees on the estate that survived thanks to him. When she passed, he was the only one willing to stay on and work with Bethany now that she's decided to renovate the estate."

"Will Bethany live here then?" I asked, thinking of the huge place and one person living there.

"She's mentioned possibly living here, but I think she's hoping to turn this into an artist's retreat," Maggie said. "I'm not sure what that means. Business was never my thing. I can organize you ten ways to heaven, but I don't have a head for the creativity and original thinking it takes to make a business go."

Even though I hadn't known her for long, I suspected if Maggie had a brainstorm, she'd be able to get any business off the ground. I would be surprised if everything wasn't organized and perfect.

"We eat at six. No dressing up, of course, because who would want to in this place?" Maggie laughed.

I laughed with her.

I glanced at the clock, which was an alarm clock, I noticed, perhaps because nothing worked quite right here.

"The clock has a battery backup. All of them in the house do," Maggie said, catching my eye.

I had a little over an hour until I needed to go down.

"Kitchen is just to the left when you get to the bottom of the stairs. Go through it and the dining room is on the other side," Maggie said as she left the room.

Behind her I thought I saw another shadow, but it was just Jimmy bringing up a box and the last of my bags.

"Is it okay if I leave that last box for the night? The rain is really starting to come down."

"That's fine," I said. "And do you know where the library is, where I'll be working?" I asked.

"You won't want to go there this late. We have the electric lanterns and stuff, but everyone tends to avoid the main part of the house when it's this dark," Jimmy said. His face reddened a little.

I didn't quite know what to say to that.

"Nathan will probably take you there to-morrow and then he can also explain what they hope you can do. I've noticed that there seems to be a lot of explaining that needs to be done," Jimmy said. He smiled when he said it, to show that it wasn't actually a criticism.

"Thank you for bringing things up for me. I'm sure this will be fine for tonight," I said.

He nodded and shut the door as he left. I saw there was a key in that nice new lock on the door.

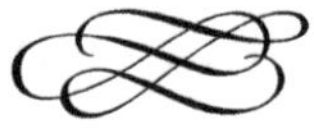

CHAPTER 4

I wanted to shower but didn't think I quite had enough time and wasn't sure I wanted to get too comfortable that close to dinner. Instead I washed my face and unpacked some of my clothing and toiletries. Thunder rumbled outside, and I heard the tapping of rain on the glass of the windows next to the bed.

My room had a radiator and it hissed when I turned up the temperature a bit. I hoped that that would be okay. I smelled the faintest acrid smell when I turned it up, as if this wasn't something that had been done often. I turned it back down, getting another blast of hissing and spitting and a slight squeak at the wheel. It was the only noise that didn't bother me.

I wondered whether I'd be in charge of cleaning my room or if Maggie had someone who would do that. I had heard there was a staff of some sort that lived on site, too. Thunder crashed loudly overhead and made me jump. The tapping at the window became a pounding fist rather than a polite clink.

The lights flickered. I opened the wardrobe intending to put away a couple of shirts and was glad to see an electric lantern sitting on the top shelf. I pulled it down and set it next to the bed. If the storm was coming up, I wanted to be able to see to find my way around.

I went over to the window to see out and watch the storm, but it was too dark to really do so. There was a faint glow coming from below me, but other than that there were no lights that I could see at all. It would be an amazing place to check out the stars on a clear night.

I thought I saw a shadow move down near the wing I was in, close to the light, but then it moved into the darkness where I could see nothing. Perhaps it was Jimmy, outside again, running an errand, or another one of the staff. Still, I thought there had been something furtive about the movements.

I drew back from the window, smiling to myself, thinking that I was doing my best to scare myself. Next thing you knew, I'd have Hercule Poirot down in the drawing room solving a murder. It was that kind of place.

It was nearly six, so I left the room, taking my key and putting the walkie-talkie in the pocket of the sweater I had on, and followed the hallway to the stairs. I went down those stairs and then made a left turn. The kitchen was there, through a large archway. The hall continued down into the dark, and I wondered what was beyond the kitchen. Perhaps another day I could explore.

The kitchen itself was huge. It was larger than my condo, which was not a small place by any means. I could easily picture this place having a couple of large fireplaces to cook over rather than the mid-twentieth century appliances they had now. The floor had a vinyl covering that had likely once had a color but was now sort of gray but for the worn parts which were black.

The cupboards were a dingy white. Many of the doors hung at awkward angles. If not for that, one could say the wood was fashionably distressed. The refrigerator was white with a small freezer on the top, and the stove was an odd sort of pink that I hadn't seen before. I breathed in deeply, enjoying the smell of fresh bread and the scent of something savory and warming.

A woman and a man were there. He was chopping something. She had her back to me at the sink. He looked up and gave me a slight smile and nodded at the door closest to me which would nearly take me back the way I had come. There were several other doors around the room as well, leading to places I couldn't see into.

I went through the door the man had nodded to and entered the dining room. Hall would have been a good word to describe this room. It was an enormous rectangular room, so vast that the lights over the large table didn't illuminate the shadows in the corners. Like everything else, it was decorated in dark paneling. Thank heavens they'd had to remove that in the bedroom when they'd redone the plumbing and wiring.

The floor was wood. While the finish was worn, it wasn't completely gone. I wondered if the room was that little used or if someone had refinished it this century. The table that sat in the middle, with two men already seated, looked to be wood as well. While most tables are made of wood, or at least finished to look like wood, I was feeling as if it might have been nice to have a different texture in here.

Maybe the decorators thought the metal candle holders in the center of the table were enough? It was hard to say. Those did sort of match the cheap looking chandeliers that hung over the table.

"Lara!" Nathan stood up. He was shorter than I expected after our Skype interviews. His hair wasn't quite as shiny black either, more a deep brown. All the same I recognized him easily.

"It's good to meet you in real life," I said, smiling.

Nathan nodded. "Maggie and Jimmy said you were here. This is Jonathan." He pointed to a tall thin man with pale blue eyes and nondescript brown hair. His face was scared, probably from acne, but I couldn't help but think they looked like claw marks.

"Jonathan is the art historian we have evaluating the art work," Nathan said the two of us had greeted each other.

"Bethany and Rachel aren't down yet," Nathan said. "Take a seat anywhere. We normally sit up towards this end. Maggie and Jimmy gravitate towards the far end. Most the people who keep up the place and eat with us will be down towards their end."

I nodded, thinking that the dining placement sounded downright like a medieval castle with the highest ranking of us towards the head of the table and the lower rank further down.

"So what do you think of the place, so far?" Jonathan asked.

"It's big," I said, trying to smile and think of something else good to say.

"It's certainly that!" A woman looking barely old enough to be called a woman and not a girl said as she walked with a definite spring to her step. Wild brown curls flowed everywhere, and I pictured her in a yellow sundress bouncing across a meadow. Tonight, though, she was in blue jeans and a red t-shirt smudged with dust and some dirt. Beneath that was a picture of two cats across the front, or perhaps bunnies. It was that dirty.

Maggie was correct to say no one dressed for dinner.

"Bethany!" Nathan said, standing again and pulling her towards me. "I want you to meet Lara Rochester."

"Lovely to meet you," Bethany said. Her smile seemed a little too big and too bright, but there was something likable about her.

She took the seat next to Nathan and I sat on his other side. Jonathan remained on the far side of the table. Maggie came in next, nodding at me, and sat down a few places down from us on the same side as Jonathan. I wondered if I should go over there, but Nathan had said this was how people were seated.

I was introduced to a couple of other people who filed in. They, too, were dusty, wearing heavy canvas overalls.

"You don't normally stay," Bethany said to one of the men, Dave, I think,

"Have you seen that rain?" Dave asked.

"Rather chance your ghosts and ghoulies than that out there tonight."

Bethany laughed. "Don't scare Lara. This is her first night at Schilling."

I smiled a little.

Dave nodded but didn't retract his statement, which seemed to put Bethany out.

The man and woman from the kitchen brought out three large bowls of salad and put them in the center of the table. I looked at our place settings, noticing we had plain white solid dishes, a small dish, probably for salad, a larger one for the main course, and a very small one that could be for bread, although I wasn't certain. There were three glasses, two of them wine glasses and one plain one along with a coffee mug, not a fancy place setting mug, but a large mug that could hold enough coffee to keep you awake most of the night.

Nathan passed the first bowl to Bethany who took some and then passed it to me. I placed mine on the small plate, just like she did, and passed the bowl back to Nathan who then passed it across to Jonathan.

A few more people came in, dressed in work clothes, the cream coveralls and heavy boots suggested they were working construction. Jimmy followed them, hurrying along to his seat.

An older woman followed. She was dressed in

baggy blue jeans and a pair of black boots and a plain blue sweatshirt.

"Sorry. Sorry," she said, sitting down to eat, as we were all taking our first bites.

The dressing was a vinaigrette with herbs. Not my first choice as I'm a creamy ranch kind of girl, but it was tasty enough. And probably kept better in that small refrigerator. If they made it fresh, the oil and vinegar could stay in the cupboards and leave more space for other things.

While we were serving, large pitchers of water and couple of opened bottles of wine were set out as well.

"This is Rachel," Nathan said when he finished chewing. "She's valuing the antiques in the house."

"Nice to meet you," I said.

"Me, too," Rachel returned and went back to dishing up salad. A lot of salad. I wondered if that was all she was going to eat. She was a tiny woman, almost birdlike, and her hair was more gray than brown. The lines on her face weren't acne scars but age lines. She wore no glasses, which surprised me, but lots of people used eye surgery now to avoid them.

"Tomorrow after breakfast, I'll take you to the library," Nathan said. "And get you settled in on what we have going on."

"I'm perfectly capable of valuing old books," Rachel said. "It's my job."

"I prefer to have more of an expert," Bethany said in a voice of quiet authority.

Rachel humphed and went back to her salad.

"You also think you can value the artwork," Jonathan replied, as if worried I'd be stung by Rachel's remark. It was rather sweet of him, although I didn't need his help.

"I'm perfectly capable of that," Rachel said. "I know several experts who would be willing to assist me." She didn't appear to notice she had just brought Jonathan's credentials into question.

"Which is why I hired Jonathan," Bethany said. "Because he is an expert."

Rachel shrugged and continued to eat.

Nathan said nothing, but I could feel tension radiating off of him.

"So how was your drive?" Bethany said, changing the subject to something less charged, or at least I hoped it was less charged.

I gave her a quick overview of the drive and how lovely I found Nova Scotia in general. That turned the conversation to the beauty of the area and soon enough the salad bowls were removed and two large platters of chicken breasts were brought out along with bowls of rice, broccoli, and carrots.

I noticed that Jonathan took the carrots but

not the broccoli. Rachel took a bit of everything but the chicken. Bethany took some of everything. I glanced down the table at the others who were digging into everything and grabbing what they needed.

Rachel poured herself a glass of wine. Bethany had already done so and was sipping at hers. Rachel seemed to gulp hers down. I tried not to show my shock.

No one else seemed horrified by that, but she didn't immediately pour another one. She was definitely an odd duck, I thought.

As we were finishing our main course, the lights flickered. Then they went out.

I paused, listening.

"Wait for it," Nathan said. There was a certain humor in voice.

The lights flickered again but it fell dark almost immediately.

"The storm," Maggie said from her end of the table. "We'll need the lanterns."

I heard a chair scrape. The lights flickered for an instant. It was long enough that I saw Bethany standing up. She grabbed something as the darkness fell again.

A fire flared as she flicked the lighter she had grabbed from the center of the table near one of the candle holders. She began lighting candles.

Down at her end, with the faint light to see by, Maggie lit her own candles.

"The generator for the kitchen is still working," the man said coming through the door. He had a flashlight and I saw electric lanterns lit in the other room.

Clearly no one thought the lights were coming back on.

"Thank you," Nathan said. "Last time, the darned thing clonked out and we lost everything we had in that refrigerator."

"Not that we keep much in there or even in the freezer out in the shed," Bethany said. "It's too unreliable. We get deliveries every other day. If you need something from the grocer, give it to Pat to put on the list."

Pat was, I assumed, one of the kitchen workers. Given that the name was rather unisex, I wasn't sure which one.

I just nodded, having just put a piece of chicken in my mouth. The sauce was very good, with a nice hint of spice but not overdone. Everything else was plain but tasty, and I could see myself eating well here.

The lights flickered again and this time they stayed on. No one reached to douse the candles.

"You never know," Nathan said. "It's why we have those electric lanterns everywhere. The electricity here is very finicky."

"So's the heat," Rachel said quietly. "You'll be going along, doing your thing and suddenly it's freezing. If I believed in ghosts…"

"Which you don't," Bethany said quickly and smiled. It seemed to me that she smiled a little too brightly. I wondered if she were trying to hide something from me.

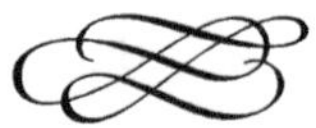

Dinner didn't last much longer. There were cookies or fruit, or both, for dessert. I had one of the oatmeal cookies. There was a hint of cardamom in them which gave them an unusual flavor that I couldn't decide if I liked or not. But they smelled heavenly and were still warm, as if they weren't long from the oven.

Nathan stood after wolfing down a cookie and said he was going up for the night. A few of the workers were also getting up and leaving, mostly in a group.

"You won't want to go alone," Rachel said, looking at me.

"Excuse me?" I asked, wondering where exactly I wasn't going to go alone to.

"Back to your room." Her tone made me feel

rather foolish for not understanding. I wondered if she were one of those people who worked very hard to be hateful.

"It's okay," Bethany said. "It's just that most of us have gotten into the habit of making sure we always have someone around. It's like the walkie-talkies. Odd things happen and you get turned around and suddenly you're wandering around the house with no idea where you are. I don't remember it happening when Aunt Audra was alive, but it seems to happen all the time now."

"The house probably hates that you're doing all the renovations," Rachel said. "Old houses are temperamental." She eyed Bethany for a second before adding, "And so are their ghosts."

Bethany drew in a breath and sighed loudly. "I'm up, then."

I stood to follow her. I noticed that Rachel didn't take her own advice, although there were still a few of the construction folks huddled around the cookies and fruit. The kitchen workers had settled with them and there were six of them or more sitting down there, and that group included Jimmy. Maggie had left with an earlier group. I wondered if she stayed on the premises or if she lived off site.

Noticing me looking, Jimmy gave me a smile and a wave and I returned it. Still, I followed

Bethany up the stairs. Jonathan was just ahead of her going quietly on his own.

"Don't let Rachel bother you," Bethany said.

"I won't. I've worked with enough people to know when someone is trying to be difficult."

Jonathan chuckled up ahead. "Rachel doesn't try. She just is."

"Poor Nathan has had his hands full with her," Bethany said. "But she is very good at what she does."

"So she says," Jonathan added.

The floor creaked when he reached the top and stepped off into the hallway. The lights were flickering here, undecided if they would stay on or go off.

"Make sure your electric lantern is close to the bed," Bethany said. "With the storm tonight, I wouldn't be surprised if the lights go out. In a new place that can be frightening."

Jonathan shivered extravagantly and un-locked a door on the left side of the hallway. The next door was Nathan's and mine was across the way, just far enough up that the doors weren't ex-actly across from each other. Bethany kept walking.

I fiddled with my key, working to get it inserted in the lock. Bethany was four doors up. I won-dered what her room was like. Finally I got the key to turn and the door to open. I felt for a light switch as the room was darker than I would have thought given the lights in the hallway.

When the lights did come on, I was disappointed in how dim they were. The light barely broke a circle on the floor. I closed the door softly and went to the bedside and lighted one of the lamps. That did better, but only just. Very little of the light hit the ceiling but at least I could see around the bed.

The pale floral patterned wallpaper looked like peeling paint in the poor light, and I wondered if that's what this room had looked like before Bethany had started making changes. It was easy enough to interpret it that way.

I crossed to the bathroom and turned on the light there. This one was brighter, or perhaps it was all the white subway tile that reflected what little light there was. I went back to the bedroom to undress and then took the electric lantern with me while I took a shower to wash the road dirt from my body and perhaps perk up my mind. There had been too much talk of ghostly intruders.

The water was deliciously hot. Perhaps there was a special water heater just for the showers. I was tempted to stay a long time but had no idea how much hot water there was. If the power went out overnight, I didn't want the others to be too angry with me for using it all up.

Fortunately the lights didn't go off while I was in there.

I padded back to the bedroom. It was a pleasant enough room and I could see it being an artist's retreat one day. The rooms were unique and probably all had an antique or two in them, especially if there weren't any closets. All they really needed was a nice big comfortable chair, although that would make the room itself a bit crowded. I wondered if there was a sitting room of some sort around.

I was lost in my fantasies as I went looking for my phone to see if I could call Tessie. I wasn't hopeful of getting through that evening but I could at least send her a text if the lines were down. That would go through as soon as service came back up.

My purse was in the cubby where I had left it, the strap slightly protruding. I didn't recall leaving it like that. I opened my purse to find my phone, but unfortunately it wasn't there. Could I have dropped it somewhere? I didn't think so. I knew I had placed it in the pocket near the top of the purse where I always left it. I hated to be unable to find my phone.

Searching my memory, I recalled that I'd tried to read some email at the last stop I'd made. I saw myself placing it carefully in the pocket because I knew my next stop would be Schilling Manor.

Once at the Manor, I had taken my purse, zipped it up and then left the car, looking at the coming storm.

Who would take my phone and why? It seemed ridiculous. I'd locked the door when I'd gone down to dinner, so who could have gotten in?

I sighed. I hated not having the thing. My stomach tightened at the thought of being there without my phone. I could go into town and get a new one to replace it. I would look in the car, first, though, just to be certain. It was possible my purse hadn't been zipped.

Deep down I was certain I wasn't wrong about having done that. Which meant that there was someone here who wasn't completely honest. I recalled Jonathan carefully using the key to his room. I thought about the shiny new locks and how solid they were. There was definitely something going on.

I was going need to find out what that was. I considered getting dressed again and knocking on Nathan's door but that felt too much like a potential booty call. I could go down the hall to find Bethany but I wasn't sure she'd tell me anything about the place. She'd probably smile and insist that my phone was safely in my car where it had likely dropped.

I'd have to wait until morning. It wasn't like I

had expected to get a message out to Tessie anyway. I looked longingly at my computer, realizing that I didn't even know if there was wifi there and if so, what the password was. I'd done a horrible job of getting myself settled in.

At least I had the walkie-talkie if something happened in the night. I could call out to the others. Of course, I mused, finding my ereader, that assumed that one of them wasn't trying to rob me or worse.

CHAPTER 6

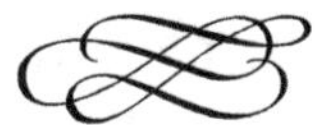

It took me longer than I wanted to fall asleep. I couldn't download a new book as I couldn't find a connection in order to download any-thing. I'd have to do it the next day. I had a few books I could read but they all seemed rather dark and gloomy, and the last thing I needed to be reading was something dark and gloomy in the manor.

I finally gave up and snuggled into the sheets, which felt soft and thick. They smelled faintly of lavender and citrus, and I suspected they were new. The blanket and comforter that was on the bed were also likely new, although they had a sort of distressed look about them, probably the better to make them fit into the place.

Not that the Ikea dressers exactly fit. They

comforted me, though, because they seemed modern and ordinary, whereas everything else seemed just a little bit skewed from normal.

Rain pattered on the window, sometimes louder and sometimes softer. The house creaked and burped. When the radiator came on, it hissed and then it spat loudly and groaned. The first time it happened, I sat bolt upright in bed wondering who was there. Images of groaning ghosts with long chains played in my mind. I turned on the light, or tried to, but the lamp wouldn't light.

It was only then that I remembered I'd left the electric lantern in the bathroom near the tub. Did I dare climb out of bed to find it?

When I banished the ghost and chains thoughts, I crawled deeper into the bed and tried to fall asleep, but it remained elusive. Each creak or groan or hiss might be a murderous ghoul about to reach out a hand and grab me. So I tossed and turned, trying to find a position that kept the noises at bay.

I finally did fall asleep but that was when the light started to come through the window and the rain had stopped pattering. Even then I dreamed that someone was walking through the room, looking around.

In my dream it was a young man in Victorian garb shaking his head and saying, "This is all wrong. Can't they see that?"

I had no idea how to help him and he drifted out of the room in my dreams and I finally slept, as if he'd taken all the ghosts with him.

I woke to the slam of a door and someone saying, "Oops, sorry!"

It sounded like Rachel, and I had a feeling she wasn't sorry at all. I slipped out of the bed now that there was enough light to see. I pulled the curtains, thankful they hadn't been pulled tightly together. That let in even more gray light. I saw sky between clouds out there, and I hoped that that meant the rain would be passing and there would be some nice weather.

When I left the bathroom, I made a point of taking the electric lantern with me and setting it carefully on the bedside table. I made up the bed and found my key. I grabbed the walkie-talkie, putting it in the pocket of my sweater. I wasn't sure I'd need a sweater but the thing was too big to fit in my jeans, which was what I was wearing.

I had on an old T-shirt that said Gamecocks. It had been a joke from Tessie because they were the main rivals of our own Clemson Tigers. It seemed like a good shirt to get filthy.

No one had said a word about breakfast. I wondered if it was a serve yourself or what. I locked my door carefully and went downstairs to see what was happening.

The stairs seemed to creak less in the morning

light. The paneling was just as dreary as ever, and I couldn't imagine a day when it wasn't depressing.

Downstairs I walked through the kitchen. The two workers were sitting around on tall stools, leaning over one of the central counters.

"Morning," I said. "Did I miss breakfast?"

The woman shook her head. "It's a buffet serve yourself out there. Different people eat at different times in the mornings."

"Ah. Thank you," I said. "Maggie didn't mention that. I'm Lara, by the way."

The woman nodded. "Pat."

"Nice to meet you."

"Bob," the man said offering a fairly limp handshake.

They both looked nice. I had more questions but they had seemed comfortable talking and resting on their stools in the kitchen drinking coffee, so I just went out to the dining room.

Rachel was there, in the same seat from the evening before. Nathan was also there and Jimmy and a young woman who was dressed in construction cream.

"Morning," I said when Nathan caught my eye.

Rachel said nothing but Nathan nodded in my direction. He gestured to the wall next to the door where I saw a sideboard loaded with food.

I had my choice of muffins, one of which looked like whole grain and another that looked like blueberry. There were several different cereals in little boxes and a pitcher of milk. Next to that was a round heating pan that held oatmeal.

There was second pan that held link sausages which smelled heavenly. A chilled bowl held more fruit. A plate held cheeses and there were jars of jams and peanut butter along with bread and a toaster. Apparently we were allowed to use the toaster without supervision.

I dished up some oatmeal and took some of the sausage and fruit. My stomach growled. I walked back to the table and saw the huge mugs which reminded me of coffee.

Reading my mind Nathan said, "Coffee and tea are off to the right." I looked where he pointed and saw that on the other side of the door was a little table in the alcove that held two of the large upright metal containers that hotels often used to serve coffee and hot water. I noticed there was no decaf on the table.

I filled the extra-large mug all the way up, thankful that it was as large as it was, and went back to dig into my breakfast.

Nathan was still snacking on toast and fruit. Rachel had a bunch of sausages which she was cutting into tiny pieces. It surprised me because watching her eat last night I had thought she was a vegetarian. Perhaps she just didn't like chicken.

"When you're done, I'll take you to the library," Nathan said. He didn't seem like he was in any hurry. In fact, when I was mostly through my oatmeal, he got another large mug of coffee and sat down to have some more.

The caffeine helped me wake up, at least a little.

"There's going to be fog later on," Rachel announced.

"How do you know?" I asked. There were no windows in the dining hall. It wasn't as if I could go look out.

Rachel shrugged. "Sometimes you just know."

"Are you from this area?" I persisted.

Rachel gave me a long look. "I'm from Chicago, although I often spend time wherever I'm needed to authenticate antiques."

"It must be very interesting." I was trying to be pleasant.

Rachel shrugged and then pushed her plate away. "I'll be working on the second floor of the main wing. I'll meet with Bethany around four. She can let you know what sorts of assistance I'll need then." She was clearly talking to Nathan and acting as if I didn't exist.

Nathan nodded at her. As Rachel exited the door through the far end, the one that lay in shadow, Jonathan came through the kitchen door. He nodded at us before going straight for the coffee urn. He was already carrying a mug, although his looked different from those here. I suspected it was a personal cup.

I finished my breakfast and leaned back to enjoy the coffee. There was little conversation. Clearly the people here were not morning people.

As I drank the last of my coffee, Nathan said, "Shall we get started or do you need another cup?"

"I'm good but I think I'd like to go out to my car. I seem to be missing my phone," I said.

"I'll go with you and then we can go to the library," Nathan said.

Nathan led the way back through the kitchen. Pat and Bob were busy at the sink, their backs to us.

"How long has Bethany been working on the estate?" I asked.

"She officially inherited at the end of last year. Audra had died probably six months before that but the tax people wanted a general valuation of the inheritance," Nathan said.

I nodded, wondering how that worked. We reached the outer door. Nathan pushed it open for me and then stepped back.

"Now she wants to know what's here and what's still in good condition. Audra let the place fall to ruin. She suffered from depression most of her life, although it was only in the last few years that anyone diagnosed it."

Interesting.

"You'll be cataloging things and making specific valuations on each book. I'll have paperwork for you from the estimator that came through for the taxes. He was valuing the collection as a whole. You'll be going book by book and then cataloging them into some sort of order. There may be several collections. There's a lot of books and all of them are old. I'm sure there are those that can be repaired, those that are in good condition and are interesting, and those that need to be tossed," Nathan said.

I shuddered in horror at the thought of tossing out books, although I knew that sometimes you had to. In a place like this, mold was likely to be an issue.

The gravel crunched under our heels. The air smelled fresh, the way it does after a storm. The sky was light and bright but off in the distance I saw more clouds. I wondered if they were coming our way.

"Later on, if it doesn't get foggy, it's a lovely walk down that path." Nathan pointed out a narrow trek that I hadn't noticed when I parked. It seemed to circle around nothing at all, but generally heading away from the Manor. It looked rather barren to me and not terribly inviting.

I got to my car. The box Jimmy had left was still in there. I had my keys. I opened the door and looked in the front. My phone was nowhere to be found.

I stood up, looking perplexed.

"What's wrong?" Nathan asked.

"I thought, in fact I was sure, I had my phone in my purse when I came here. But it's not there and it's not in the car," I said.

"Let's look a little harder first," Nathan said. I opened the passenger side and we searched around the floors and under the seats. As expected the phone wasn't there, though I did find a few stray French fries, which were probably the reason for the odor in my car. I looked under the backseat, moving around the one lone box, but still nothing.

I stood up shaking my head. Nathan looked troubled.

"I hate to think someone would have stolen it. They'd have to have had a key, wouldn't they?"

"I don't recall leaving the door unlocked," I said. "And I was there except when I went down to dinner." I didn't mention that I'd taken a shower, not liking the idea that someone could have slipped in and taken something.

Nathan rubbed his chin but nodded. "We've

had a few tools go missing but it always seemed like something being misplaced. Well, and the art restorer before Jonathan lost his phone as well. That's when we upgraded the locks on the doors."

Nathan paused for a bit, staring off into space. Finally he added, "Did you have a case so you can describe it for me?"

I gave him the make and model and then described the case I had, colored in Clemson orange and purple with the Tiger on the back.

We had walked back to the door. "That should stand out," Nathan said. "I'll call for Maggie and see what she says."

We went inside, Nathan picking up the walkie-talkie that sat by the backdoor. I noticed he had one in his pocket but chose not to use it. I glanced in the kitchen. Pat and Bob weren't anywhere to be seen.

Behind me, Nathan was talking to Maggie. I couldn't quite hear what was being said on her end. There was a lot of static and I had to wonder where she was.

"Maggie said she'll have the housekeepers keep an eye out for it," Nathan said. "And everyone else."

"Thanks."

"I hate to think that someone here would steal something."

"I was hoping it would be in the car," I said. "Then it would have been a non-issue."

"I suppose if Jimmy saw it on the ground and picked it up, it could be somewhere else in your room?"

I thought about it, but couldn't imagine where he'd have put it. I'd gone through my suitcases. I'd even looked in a couple of the boxes on the top. It didn't seem very likely.

"Well, let's go to the library, then." Nathan set off through the dining hall. Bethany gave us a wave and then went back to her meal. Jonathan was still there. Now, instead of coffee, he had a big plate of food in front of him.

We exited through the far door which took us to a wide corridor covered, like everything else, in dark wood paneling. There were lights here but they struggled to hold back the shadows. It wasn't a place I'd want to walk through in the dark. It was bad enough walking through it in the daylight.

The corridor ended in a narrower hallway which, to our right, opened into the main entrance. The cheap doors I had noticed before looked even more out of place in here. There was plain drywall around them, as if someone was working on changing things but hadn't finished. The white paint on them was just too bright in comparison.

"The old doors were twice as tall and we were having a hard time finding something to replace them. Audra had let things get so deteriorated that water was coming in the front when the storms blew in from the sea," Nathan said. "We had to do something for now. Bethany and her designers are trying to decide the best option."

Across from the doors, past a large open space that would have held the average living room, spiraled a long stairwell. The entry was open up through the next two floors and an old chandelier hung there. It was high enough that I wasn't sure if it had lights or candles. The wooden rail on the stairwell had been painted white once but was now chipped and poor looking.

"The stairs are solid, although the rail isn't in very good condition," Nathan said. "Bethany worries it's an accident waiting to happen, and she's right, but we haven't decided how accurately to portray the entry. Originally it was all dark wood, but in her younger years Audra had this idea that she'd paint things white and brighten the manor up. She got through the stairwell and that was it."

It made me sad to think of a woman who had lived here all her life making plans for something that never happened, just giving up. Of course, I had sort of done that myself and if not for Tessie, perhaps I'd still be doing that.

A shadow flickered off to my left but when I

turned in that direction, I saw nothing there. A moment later, the room got very chill. I felt my arms break out in goose bumps as I pulled my sweater closer around me. Nathan shivered and then walked quickly across the hall.

"One of those moments that Rachel talked about," he said. "We've got to install better heating."

"I don't see any radiators here," I said.

"There's an oil furnace that runs the main wing," Nathan said. "It's actually up to code. Audra lived mostly in six or seven rooms on the second floor of this wing."

I had this desire to go see those rooms, to see how that woman had lived. I didn't ask though my curiosity about her was aroused.

We'd crossed the great hall and were in another large room. This was clearly the library. It was lined with books on dark wood shelves and there was a second floor catwalk that lined the room. A metal spiral stair waited in one corner for those who wanted to reach the higher shelves. A couple of dark wood ladders leaned against the walls, on a track so it would be easy to move them. In the center of the room were a dozen or so low shelves all filled with books. There was no carpet here, although in the corner I saw something rolled up. I wondered why that had been done. I hoped it wasn't because of dampness.

Mold is the bane of old books, and archivists hate it the way other people hate spiders. The only thing worse was fire, but at least fire was quick. Mold was a slow death for a book.

Against the wall to the left, looking out to the front of the Manor, were two long windows with floor length drapes in heavy dark velveteen that had gone nearly black through the years. After all, who would want bright colors anywhere in the house? Audra didn't seem to be the only one who was depressed in the family.

"Let's go upstairs to Audra's library," Nathan said.

"Her library?" I asked. I had been told she had a personal library, but I was thinking of a few shelves. Suddenly, that seemed rather naïve.

"You'll see," Nathan said.

He led me up the great staircase, staying close to the wall. I followed suit, just to be safe. At some point this place had been beautiful, and I hoped that Bethany was able to make it beautiful again. She'd started work there, clearly. The wood had been sanded, though not redone. It appeared that someone had pulled down wallpaper as there were spots of it here and there.

"We need to redo wiring before we can redo the walls," Nathan said. "But the electrician has to plan out where to put lights. We had to work hard to get him to sort out the rooms we're in in the east wing."

When we finally got to the top of the stairs, I smelled rotten food. It was just a whiff and then it seemed to be gone.

Nathan led me down a hallway that led to the left. Audra's library was only a few doors down and faced the back of the manor. It had two large windows looking out and no curtains. The floor here had been sanded down and from the looks of it, boards had been replaced, recently.

The walls here were lined with shelves in dark wood. Small stools sat around the room and there was a large overstuffed sofa in a heavy tapestry-type upholstery. It was gray with age, though I could see faint traces of patterns that suggested there had once been flowers. A matching chair sat next to one of the windows. A spot on the floor suggested there had been a table there.

"It's much smaller, but still a good number of books," Nathan said.

I agreed. The room was probably ten feet by twenty, and the walls, except for where the windows were and the main door, were lined with books. There was no fireplace in this room and if I recalled, I didn't remember seeing one downstairs. Clearly whoever cared for the books was afraid they'd burn if there was a fire around.

"And there's the schoolroom."

Nathan smiled as I was mentally calculating the numbers in here.

We went back out and climbed the stairs to the third floor. I heard someone pounding on something, probably a worker. It was distant.

"More work on the east wing," Nathan said. "It's a bit easier to work with as it's more modern. That way Bethany can have people staying on site as they continue to work on the main wing."

We went across a catwalk that looked down over the stairs to the entry and passed a closed door on my right. The next door we came to, Nathan opened.

The schoolroom. This was done in a lighter wood. The paneling had darkened with age but at one time it had been a knotty sort of pine. Perhaps cheaper and easier to replace. I couldn't be certain. It was packed with boxes, and from the openings I saw books.

"This is where they'd started packing up the old books they didn't know what to do with," Nathan said. "The boxes closest to the door are old paperbacks that Audra probably purchased. As you go further back, you start seeing older books."

I nodded. In addition to mold and mildew I started to think about mice and insects. This was going to be a mess. The books in these boxes could take me years to catalog, and they wanted me to have it done in six months to a year. I recalled something about a few boxes. How could anyone misrepresent this huge room full of boxes as a 'few'?

Looking at all of them, I started to feel a bit like Cinderella.

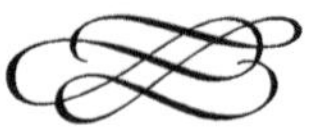

CHAPTER 7

Nathan led me back down the stairs and to the library. I was going to need a map for all the places we'd been. At least the library didn't smell quite so moldy. It smelled drier, although whether that was a good thing or not remained to be seen. If the books had absorbed all the moisture I was smelling earlier, that could be a bigger problem than I expected.

The rolled-up carpet worried me. Nathan saw me eyeing it.

"It wasn't wet," he said. "It was just stained and worn. We need to get someone to pull it out of here."

That made me feel slightly better.

Hidden at the far end of the library was a large desk. Nathan showed me notes from the estate appraiser. Below and around the desk were boxes from various office supply stores full of sticky notes, index cards, pens, and even some paper. There was a surprisingly new-looking working computer on the desk along with a printer. Extra sticky labels sat beside it.

"You'll find software on the system that catalogs books," Nathan said. "It's probably not university standard or anything, but it should work for what we need. If you need to upgrade it to something more, please come and talk with me."

I nodded. "What about the internet? I know there's poor connectivity here."

"This is on a buried cable which we had installed, and it cost a fortune. If any computer can get out, this one can."

"What about a password to the internet in case I want to work up in my room?"

Nathan wrote down a string of letters and numbers on a piece of paper. I took it and put it in my sweater pocket near my walkie-talkie and thanked him. We talked for some time about the job and the expectations. The building creaked and groaned around us but other than that it was silent in that part of the Manor.

Nathan left, leaving me alone in the large room, which was suddenly too silent. It was like the house was checking me out, all the creaks and groans paused while it did so. If I had my phone I could put on music, or at least I hoped I could put on music. Perhaps there was something on the computer.

I entered the credentials I'd been given by Nathan a few moments ago and the computer came up, a pleasant and familiar sound in the waiting silence. I heard scratching from behind me. I turned while the computer finished its booting, looking around. There were books there. I considered pulling them out to see if there was a rat behind them or if there was damage to the walls, but I didn't want a wild rat running out at me.

My fingers sort of itched at the thought of the creature jumping out and scaring me like in some horror movie. The scratching sound stopped as quickly as it had started. I turned back to the computer.

I looked at the name of the catalog software. It wasn't one I was familiar with, so I got online, which was easy enough, and started reading up on it. It was primarily for home use or small libraries. I could argue that this wasn't a small library but likely it would work for what we needed.

I took a moment to send an email to Tessie so she wouldn't worry if she didn't get a phone call from me. Of course, she'd probably worry because my phone had been stolen. I was worried about that.

While Nathan might hold out the thought that it was an innocent mistake, I was fairly certain someone had purposely taken my phone. I just didn't know why.

It occurred to me that I didn't know that much about Audra Schilling. I'd looked up Schilling Manor online before arriving to find out about the family in general, seeing I'd be working for them. I knew they'd made most of their money in coal. They hadn't run any of the big coal mines that had given rise to the main towns. Instead they'd run a couple of smaller finds, one of which had run out within a year of opening.

Still, the investment in coal had paid off well enough that they had money to invest in railroads, owning a piece of every railroad they could buy. They had investments in shipping as well. There were a few rumors that not all of the fortune was above board, particularly when Audra's father, Mitchell Schilling, had been in charge, but there were no specifics, at least not in my cursory search.

Audra Schilling had been born in 1928, so she'd been nearly ninety when she died, an impressive age. She was the only child to survive. She'd had an older brother who had died before his first birthday and a younger sister who had lived only three years. There had been no more children after that.

She'd lived in the Manor with both her parents until their deaths. I couldn't find anything that suggested she'd ever been engaged, which I found strange, given the era. It made me wonder about her father. There was less information about his personal life, although I was able to find plenty on him as a businessman and investor.

If there was any information, it was likely here in the house. Had Audra not married because she didn't want to marry? Had her father kept her from marriage? He'd died suddenly in 1951, leaving everything to his daughter. Her mother had died in 1968. There was little information to be found, at least not in the cursory searches I was doing. Again, that sort of information was likely in the house.

I sighed, mentally planning my actions for the afternoon. The lights overhead flickered and died. The drapes were pulled which plunged the room into nearly complete darkness. I froze for a second, looking at the darkened computer, hoping it was plugged into a surge protector. I was thinking that perhaps a battery backup would be a good idea. That way I'd have time to save and log out of the programs I was using.

There was the thinnest line of light near one of the windows.

For a moment that light disappeared. I felt no

breeze in the room to have moved the draperies. I turned, watching.

The drapery didn't move again. I stood up to go open it, to give myself some light. I held my arms forward to make sure I didn't hit something in the darkened room. Two steps from the desk I felt like I had walked into a cold wall.

I moved backwards, wondering what it was when I felt someone touch my hand from behind.

A scream passed my lips even before I could turn. I had never considered that ghosts could touch people.

CHAPTER 8

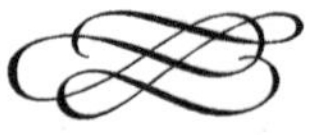

Someone else yelped, their voice lower and quieter than my own.

"Who is it?" I demanded, thinking that a ghost wouldn't have screamed because I did.

"It's Jimmy," the voice said.

"Don't you have a light?" I asked.

"I'm always leaving mine. It's not usually a problem," Jimmy said. "I was on my way here to see if you needed me to carry that last box in. I figured I'd do it before I grabbed some lunch."

"Can you get the drapes open?" I asked. "That should allow us to see each other while we speak."

I heard him move through the library. He kicked something, probably one of the low sets of shelves. Then I was able to see a shadowy outline which became clearer as he got to the window. Then he pulled the drapes. He sneezed.

The dust was so heavy I thought I would suffocate. I'd need a mask if I was going to be working in here, else I'd fall ill. I hoped I'd remembered to pack something like that or I'd be delayed in my cataloging.

"Yuck," Jimmy said. He looked gray in the light but perhaps he was just covered with that much dust.

"I'm sorry," I said. I really ought to go to his aid and open the other draperies.

"No problem," he said. "It's my job. But, if you have your keys?"

"I do," I said. "And do you need the one to the room as well?" I asked.

"Maggie gave me the master when she reminded me there was still a box in your car," Jimmy said. "So just for the car."

"Great. You can leave them in the room. Nightstand next to the bed." I figured that way there wouldn't be any questions about where he would leave them.

"Will do," he said, leaving me. "You might want to think about lunch now. The power will probably come on shortly. Chances are someone looked at a light switch wrong and it blew a fuse. That means they'll have to go down to the basement and figure out which fuse, and that can take a bit."

"Maybe I'll do that," I said. I followed him out of the library and back into the dining hall. I considered going back to my room and washing up but maybe I'd just ask if I could use the kitchen sink. I continued through and saw Pat and Bob slicing bread.

"Can I wash my hands in the sink?" I asked.

"If you go out near the side door there's a powder just to the other side," Pat said. "Probably a bit nicer than this old sink. They replaced those pipes and it's not so noisy."

"Thanks," I said and continued out around the hall. I saw the stairs and went by those. I figured there ought to be a door soon enough and there was. It was a larger room than I'd have expected of a bathroom. I wondered what it had been originally. Surely there hadn't been bathrooms when the place was built, were there?

It was all tile, but regular square tile in a gray white that suggested this particular powder room had been around for a number of years. It was very clean, though, and the toilet looked new. The walls had the same tile halfway up, giving the place a rather industrial look, but perhaps this was the powder room Audra's household help had used.

The sink dripped for about thirty seconds after

I turned off the faucet and then I smelled something that I can only describe as nearly drowned rat. I suppose what I was smelling was wet hair, perhaps having washed down that drain at some point, but it made me think of rats in sewers. I wrinkled my nose. Here I was going to lunch. Lucky me.

I wandered back out and into the dining hall. Several of the construction workers were at the far end of the table. I was surprised at how bright it was, but apparently the fuse box only connected to the rooms in the main house and not this wing. This area had lights.

The table seemed even longer than it had the night before, perhaps a factor of having more light. It was certainly larger than any table I'd seen, even in a place like the Biltmore, where you could tour the dining room.

I grabbed the mug by my place and filled it with coffee. None of the people at my end of the table were there yet so I made my way down to the foot of the table and started talking to the two men and one woman who were eating sandwiches from brown bags.

"Don't they provide you with lunch?" I asked.

One of the men shrugged. "We can get it here, but after a time it starts tasting all the same."

The woman nodded. "Sometimes I eat here.

Sometimes I bring something. Sometimes a little of both, I guess."

"You the new one?" the third man asked.

I said I was. "Where are you working now?"

"We're up on the third floor, probably above the rooms you're in. We're finishers, mostly. There are teams outside, too. A whole group of roofers. And one working on that old greenhouse which has been nothing but a headache since day one."

The woman nodded. "They don't like it out there. The glass keeps getting damaged but no one can figure out why. They've reordered about three times."

That was odd.

"And they don't know why?" I asked.

Everyone shook their heads.

"Sabotage?"

The woman shrugged.

"Who'd want to?" one of the men said. He chewed a bite quickly before saying anything else. "It's not like there was anyone but Bethany to inherit, and if she does make this an artist's retreat, it would offer some jobs around here, year round probably."

Who would want to sabotage indeed? But he hadn't said it was. Of course, no one had said it wasn't either.

"I was in the library earlier," I said. "Working. When the lights went off I went to open the drapes but I thought I'd walked into a wall of cold. Does that kind of thing happen often?"

"All the walls here are pretty cold when you think about it." The talkative man laughed. The other nodded.

"It was in the middle of the room," I said. I wasn't in the mood for joking. I wanted a good answer.

"We've all felt the cold," the woman said. "It just comes and goes. No one has a good reason for it, except maybe a ghost. You know there are cold spots in haunted houses and stuff."

"So you think it's ghosts?"

"Can't find a better reason for the cold spots," the man said. "No one described it like a wall though."

Which meant no one had run into something large and cold, they'd only felt cold. I'd felt something like a body frozen in ice, which was maybe why I kept calling it a wall. Because I didn't even want to think about a frozen body. I shivered, gripping my coffee mug for the warmth. I let the scent waft up into my nose, bringing me back to the table.

I let the conversations buzz around me while I drank, hoping that I could caffeinate my fears away. It wasn't working and I was getting hungry.

Jonathan came into the dining hall and started picking at the food. He hadn't noticed me sitting down at the end of the table so I got up, placing my mug at my seat and went up behind him. I was surprised when he jumped a little.

"Sorry. I didn't mean to startle you."

"Just been working alone for the whole morning," he said. "I'm going through some of the artwork that was stored in the attic. There's no electricity up there at all so I'm working under battery operated lights. There's so much dust and rat droppings that I'm amazed that any of the artwork up there is salvageable at all. The only good thing is that I got to explore the widow's walk, which they've already made sure was safe."

I picked up a bowl and took some of the soup. It smelled like an ordinary chicken noodle but that would do.

"How was your morning? Other than not finding your phone?" Jonathan asked when he sat down again.

I was a little surprised that he'd heard about my phone but perhaps everyone had. We were all on the same channel on the walkie-talkies.

"I was just getting started in the library when the power went out there," I said. "Jimmy was coming by to move another box out of my car when it happened and he said it might take some time to sort it out."

Jonathan nodded but didn't say anything else. "You know, Nathan and Bethany hate it when we talk like this, but I swear this place doesn't want to give up any of its secrets. If I believed in ghosts, well, I'd have left after the first day. You know, I'm the second art historian to have worked here and Rachel is the third antiques person."

"How many librarians?" I asked, smiling a little, although the fact that there had been other people working here gave me a bit of a start.

"Only you," Jonathan said. "Originally they had found someone who specialized in art and rare books and thought that was enough, but the project is so huge and finding people who would stay so difficult that they decided to chop up the jobs. Rachel may be willing to do all our jobs, and the way things are going, she might end up with that, although it will take her forever. I think she's gotten through about a third of what the previous dealer got through in a day and she's been here for two weeks."

"How long have they been working on sorting things?" I asked.

"Since Audra Schilling died," Jonathan said. "Now, this is all gossip because I listen and the people down at the little cove town like to gossip, but apparently there's been nothing but trouble since Audra died. The house was in disrepair for half her life but it wasn't weird like this, or at least not as weird. Some of that is probably trying to update the electrical panels and rewiring what they can get to, but lots of it is pretty unexplainable. People used to come up from the town to help out, moving boxes and things, but they don't do that anymore."

I sipped at my soup thinking about what Jonathan was telling me. He went on about theories and I listened with half an ear, wondering if I wanted a sandwich or something else. He had taken a bunch of meats and cheeses and crackers and was snacking on them between sharing gossip. He had a few tomatoes and radishes as well, but those were just sitting on the plate, at least so far.

"Of course, they all say that Audra's luck had always been bad," Jonathan said. The mention of Audra and something personal made my ears perk.

"What do you mean?" I asked. It was the first time I'd done anything more than murmur some sort of response since he'd begun. That seemed to get him going as he straightened up and began that story.

"You know she was engaged. Around the time of the war, of course, and her fiancé was a commoner and had fought over there but came back wounded. It didn't matter to Audra. They were 'in love.'" Jonathan made large finger quotes around the word.

"Anyway, one night he just disappeared. People said he'd left the area because he couldn't stand to be home again. I guess he'd been pretty changed—quiet and then angry and real unpredictable when he'd come home. Of course, I guess no one really knew he was a suitor. It was very scandalous as he worked for her father out here on the grounds. I guess something like Jimmy's job was for Audra."

"That's very sad," I said. And she'd never married or had another suitor. I had seen a few photos of her in my research and she wasn't an ugly woman, so she must have been devoted to the man.

Jonathan nodded. "They say that she was never the same after that, becoming quieter. Before, I guess, she was a lot like Bethany, outgoing and smiling. After her father died, I hear she became downright reclusive. She didn't particularly want to talk to anyone then, and, of course, being a rich woman, she didn't have to."

"Do you know anything more about the family itself?" I asked.

"Like what?" Jonathan asked.

"Her father maybe?"

At that moment Bethany waltzed into the room. She looked surprisingly clean in her jeans and floral print blouse. She had on a white sweater that held her walkie-talkie in the pocket. She breezed over to us as she grabbed her mug.

"I hear that Nathan got you started this morning!" She said it like it was some sort of milestone.

"A little. Unfortunately the power went out," I said. "Jimmy suggested it was a good time for lunch."

"Well, at least you can give me a few updates on what you think now that you've actually seen everything," Bethany said. "Let me get some food."

I gave Jonathan a look but he shook his head ever so slightly, as if the topic of Bethany's family was off limits when she was around.

I got up to get a bit of lunch meat—turkey for me—and a lovely looking hard roll. There was butter and mustard and some cheese. I added lettuce and quickly had a nice sandwich. There was a small broccoli salad which I took a bit of and some of the tomatoes that Jonathan had. They were the tiny grape tomatoes. I hoped they were tasty.

Bethany had already settled when I came back to the table. We spent the rest of lunch discussing what I thought of the work and how long it might take.

After listening while he finished his lunch, Jonathan got up and left for the attic once more.

At some point Nathan joined us, taking Rachel's seat rather than sitting between the two of us as he had the night before.

"Rachel will hate that," Bethany pointed out.

"When was the last time she came down when anyone was eating lunch?" Nathan asked.

Bethany sighed. I wanted to ask her about Rachel but didn't want to seem gossipy.

Several people from the construction and cleaning crews came in and left while we talked. I was starting to feel restive.

"I should see if the power is on back there," I said.

"I'm sure we can catch up again in a few days," Bethany said, still smiling.

"I'm sure."

I was barely out of the dining hall, the voices still echoing behind me, when the hallway got cold and I rubbed my arms. The light seemed to dim around me.

I heard voices from behind one of the closed doors in the corridor.

I walked slowly, trying to be quiet, although given the propensity of the floor to squeak I wasn't particularly successful. Still, the voices didn't change.

"You know the master was delighted that he disappeared," a woman said. I pushed open the door, slowly, looking around but saw no one.

I stood there, staring into the empty space, wondering where the voices were coming from. I turned to go when I thought I saw two women in uniforms that could have dressed the extras in *Downton Abby* standing near a table that hadn't been there a moment ago. When I turned again to get a good look, it was gone.

The chill intensified for a moment, like someone had opened a freezer. Just as quickly it was gone. The lights brightened around me.

I was reminded of Jonathan's comments about ghosts.

I had had my fortune told shortly after graduation. Tessie and I had thought it would be fun. The woman had looked at me and sighed. "You're sensitive," she said quietly. "You'll be the one who notices the spirits when everyone else walks on without pause."

It suddenly occurred to me that perhaps coming here was not a particularly wise decision. There was enough strangeness going on without having to see ghosts.

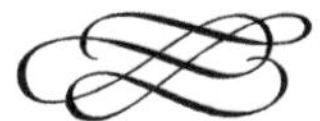

CHAPTER 9

I walked slowly back to the library. The floor still creaked. It smelled normal, the faintest hint of chicken soup, coming from behind me. I was cool but not cold or chilled, although mentally I was rather frightened. I didn't want to see a formless ghost coming towards me. I didn't want to see any ghost, really.

Coming here felt wrong. I wondered if I could use Skype on the business computer, seeing I couldn't even call a friend with my phone missing. I wanted to hear a friendly voice.

The lights were on in the library. I went to the computer and tried starting it again. It made the usual noises upon starting and I began to relax a little. Now, to decide where to begin cataloging.

I spot checked books around the room, figuring that this would be the logical room to begin with. After all, I had the computer there. The other rooms would need to be done on paper and then entered into the system. Perhaps I could ask Nathan to hire someone when I got that far, or else I'd be cataloging in the morning and entering data in the afternoon.

Looking at the layout, it appeared that the books were in no particular order. However, the oldest of them seemed to be to the left of the second window, so I began there, taking my sticky notes with me, and began the process of sorting and cataloging.

I had one color sticky notes for fiction and another for non-fiction, which would give me a very general sort of information. I was also noting what shelf each book was on so that when it came time to sort through them, I could easily find them again. Finally, I had to go through and mark what sort of condition each book was in.

It was all detail work and very time consuming. I hadn't felt as if I had been working long when I glanced up and out the window. Everything was cloudy. Rachel had been right about the fog. It made me wonder what else she might be right about.

It was a thick fog that made me glad I wasn't out driving in it. I wondered if the roads were as bad as this hill. There was little visibility and as the sun set, it would get worse. I was glad that this sort of thing didn't happen often near me.

I went back to working on my books.

"There you are!" Maggie said coming in. I'd worked my way through three more shelves and was just getting started on the fourth. I'd taken to pulling down half a shelf of books and setting them on the desk and working my way through them and then replacing them. I'd found three books that appeared to be quite valuable, and a half dozen that, while having potential value, were in such poor condition that I'd have to search out how common they were. I was leaving that task to the end. I was hoping to work up in my room after dinner

"Yes?" I asked.

"We've found your phone. Bob found it in the kitchen. It'd been kicked under one of the counters." Maggie held out the phone, the brightly familiar orange and purple clearly recognizable.

"Thank you," I said, feeling relief. That was quickly replaced by another fear. I couldn't remember being in the kitchen with my purse. How could it have gotten that far without someone noticing it and picking it up? Which meant that someone had to have taken it and perhaps left it in the kitchen to be found.

"I bet it just fell out of your purse when we

were in there," Maggie said. She was too cheerful in trying to find a logical reason.

"I don't recall that I had my purse there."

"Oh, but you did," she assured me. She was trying too hard to convince me of something I remembered very differently.

"Have there been other things going missing?" I asked.

"Well, you know how it is in construction. A tool gets misplaced here or there," she said cheerfully. "Your phone was the most concerning. I'm glad it's been found." She didn't mention anyone else missing a phone. I wondered if she really had forgotten or if there were other secrets she was keeping.

"Me, too," I said. I tried to start it and it blinked on and then off again. It was enough to tell me the battery was dead. I was going to have to charge it back in the room before it would be of much use to me. Perhaps over the weekend I'd see if there was a place in Sydney that would take a look at it for me to make sure everything was fine.

"Are you going to be here much longer?" Maggie asked.

"I wanted to finish this shelf," I said. I glanced at the clock on the computer. It wasn't near dinner, at least not yet. I had plenty of time.

"Just checking. Most of our workers left already because of the fog, so it'll be quiet here."

"Of course, no one can do something to pop one of the fuses," I said, wondering if that was the right terminology. I had always had homes with circuit breakers.

Maggie nodded. "I'll leave you to it." She seemed like she wanted to say more. I was tempted to call her back.

When she left, the room felt too quiet, too lonely. It was odd that while I had worked there alone, before she'd come in I hadn't felt bothered. I'd been busy with the books and the work. Now, I was sitting there listening to every sound, practically jumping when the floor creaked or a window groaned.

My mind wandered in a hundred different directions, and I kept looking at shadows that seemed to move out of the corner of my eye. I started to make a note three times and stopped each one because I thought I saw someone moving to my right, but no one was in the room with me.

Something started to scratch at the wall behind me. My lunch rose in my throat. It was likely a rat and I do *not* like rats.

Sitting there, trying to calm myself and hold down my food, I couldn't decide if seeing a ghost or a rat would be worse. Without being aware of it, I had put down my pen and wrapped my arms around my chest. I still had half a shelf of books to go but I couldn't make myself do anything else.

I got up and grabbed my notes, leaving the room behind. I didn't turn off the lights. They'd been on early in the morning. Quite honestly, I didn't know where the switch was, and I didn't care to go looking for it.

Maggie, or someone who worked in the house, could turn them off. If not, the power would probably fail at some point and save the estate some money.

I heard something fall upstairs. I considered going up, but there was a strange silence after the sound. I got very cold again, that iciness that seemed to come and go.

I hurried around the corner and into the hallway that led back to the dining room. Sometime when I wasn't so freaked out, I'd have to explore. No doubt the hallway on the second floor would lead around to the right and to the east wing, at least it seemed logical enough. Then I wouldn't have to go through the dining room and up to my room.

The large dining hall was empty. I heard Pat and Bob in the kitchens, their voices low as they murmured about cooking and who would chop the onion. Pots clattered against tile and wood. I smiled as I went through.

Pat nodded at me. Bob raised a hand. Considering that it held a knife, it didn't feel reassuring.

I left their soft murmurings behind as I climbed the stairs to the second floor. Someone was playing piano music in their room. Bach, if I wasn't mistaken. I wondered who was up there already.

I opened the door to my room to see that Jimmy had left the second box in the corner. I glanced at the nightstand and there were my car keys. I closed the door with a soft click and hurried over to them. I put them back in my purse, which remained in its cubby. My wallet and everything else, down to a dollar bill that I had squirreled away in an emergency pocket, was there.

I didn't hear the piano music in my room. The walls had to be thick, then.

Someone ran down the hallway, feet pounding. I stood up, wondering who was running and what was going on. The pounding feet came back down the hall and then someone banged on my door.

I hurried over to see what was going on. I pulled open the door but there was no one in the hall.

The sound of pounding steps was gone.

No one else looked out their doors, although the piano music had stopped.

I closed the door once more. I rested my back

against it, wondering what was out there. The pounding feet came again.

I considered looking out, but realized I was too frightened. My hands shook as I reached for the knob. Instead of twisting it open, I twisted the lock and backed away from the door, staring at it, willing it to stay closed.

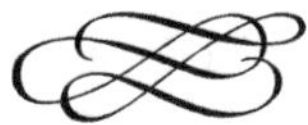

I had no idea how long I stood there. My legs were pressed against the end of the bed, my arms were folded across my chest. I listened as the pounding went back and forth along the hallway.

I finally forced myself to do something in the room. Maybe if I ignored them, the sounds would go away or at least not bother me quite so much. I plugged my phone in and grabbed my computer so I could do some research.

I settled onto the bed, piling up the pillows to make myself comfortable. I once again wished for a chair and spent a couple of moments mentally rearranging the room to make one fit. I wondered if Bethany would add one before she opened the retreat. Surely I wasn't the only one to want a chair. The others had retired early last night as well.

I hunched over my laptop and started searching out some information on a couple of books. I made a few notes on the cards I'd brought. I got lost in my research, coming up for air, so to speak, only when a door slammed.

I realized then that the sound of running, pounding feet was gone. I looked at the time. It was almost six. I wasn't late for dinner, but I needed to stop work and get going.

I checked my sweater. I had my walkie-talkie. I hesitated before the door. I drew in a breath and tried to calm my pounding heart. A shaking hand reached out to turn the knob.

It didn't move.

I felt a scream building in my throat. I pulled at the knob again, trying to make it turn. I looked more closely at it, wondering if I could find something in the room to fix it or if I'd need to call for assistance on the walkie-talkie.

The lock was still engaged from when I'd turned it earlier. I breathed out, feeling silly.

I unlocked the door, made sure I had my key, and left the room, feeling more than a little foolish. I was smiling as I walked down the hall to the stairs.

Bob and Pat were busy in the kitchen, but Pat returned my smile. Everything smelled like roasted onions and garlic. I wondered what they'd served up that night.

I crossed into the dining room. Nathan and Bethany were there, but no Jonathan or Rachel, not yet.

"Evening, Lara," Nathan said. "How's it going?"

"I got a start on things," I said.

We engaged in chitchat about cataloging books and the kinds of things I had seen on that one shelf, which was likely to be the most difficult of the sections to work on as the books there were oldest. I was also likely to find the most valuable books there, too. The boxes upstairs might contain something interesting as well, but those were far more likely to hold damaged books, having been packed away for so long.

Jonathan joined us shortly before we were once again served salad, which we all took some. The dressing was different this time, still a vinaigrette but with a slightly different spice that I couldn't identify. There was something slightly sweet in it, too.

I ate heartily, my fears from earlier forgotten, and my stomach ready to take in whatever nourishment it could. Rachel arrived about halfway through the salad. This time she barely took any and ate quickly.

"And how was your day?" Bethany asked her.

Rachel sighed, as if this question was rude or she was being put upon by being forced to answer it.

"I got Audra's sitting room finished," she said. "There was a lot of junk in there, let me tell you."

Bethany smiled a little. Neither she nor Nathan seemed all that excited.

"Do you suppose you'll be finished with her rooms by the end of the week?" Nathan asked.

"I couldn't say," Rachel said. "All of this takes up time. I need to look at everything and make notes. Sometimes I need to do research. I can eyeball things, but if you're looking for the kind of exacting inventory and evaluation you've talked about, I can't just give you a guesstimate."

"All the same," Nathan replied easily, "we're hoping that you can do your best to speed up the process."

"Maybe if the lights worked a bit better, and I didn't have to keep laying ghosts to rest, it'd be easier, but all that takes time. You'll be glad of the extra time I'm taking to do that when you open this as an artists' retreat," Rachel said with a straight face. She really did believe in ghosts.

I considered talking with her about my experiences, but that lasted perhaps half a second.

I felt Nathan draw in a breath to say something when Jonathan broke in.

"I'm not sure that the ghosts are real, and I'm

pretty sure that the areas you say you've cleared have just as much trouble as the ones you haven't," he said easily.

Rachel glared at him. "Maybe you're the one who should pay attention to your job."

"Never mind," Nathan said quickly, interrupting the two of them. Clearly they didn't particularly like each other. I couldn't exactly blame Jonathan. I didn't much like Rachel either, and her claims of laying ghosts to rest seemed far-fetched to say the least.

Jimmy hurried through the room towards the far end of the table, giving us all a wave. I smiled and gave him a little wave back. The others nodded or waved. Rachel completely ignored him, still glaring at Nathan.

Bethany changed the subject so that we were discussing the weather. I was happy to hear that there weren't any storms in the forecast, which meant, I hoped, that the power would remain on for the evening. I didn't want a repeat of the last night.

After finishing the salads, we were served large dishes of spaghetti noodles and spaghetti sauce. There were meat balls as well. I noticed that Rachel didn't have any problems taking plenty of meat to go with her meal this evening.

Jonathan ate a lot of everything, taking three pieces of the garlic bread that was served last.

I dug in, enjoying the food more than I had expected. The sauce was mild, the meatballs slightly spicy, and the garlic bread had just enough flavor to make everything perfect. I listened more than I spoke, hoping to learn something about the family. I wished they would start talking about the history of the place or perhaps Bethany's family, but the subject didn't come up. Nor was I offered any openings.

Dessert was thin slices of carrot bread or else fruit. I would have preferred carrot cake, but if you're not paying for the food, you probably didn't get a choice. It seemed that Pat and Bob used their abilities to do the cooking rather than spending time baking.

Nathan and Bethany left the table at the same time. That left me with Rachel and Jonathan, not a pair I wanted to spend too much time with. I listened in on Jimmy's discussion with Maggie about how soon they could go back to working on the roof.

None of the construction workers had eaten dinner with us this time, so the room felt nearly empty. The shadows seemed longer with so few people. I quickly finished my carrot bread and got up to go to my room.

"I'll go with you," Jonathan said, standing.

Rachel glared at him. "For someone who doesn't believe in ghosts…"

Jonathan didn't even acknowledge what she said. He followed me out through the kitchen. Pat and Bob were wiping down the counters.

"I hate it that she talks about ghosts and stuff. I mean, if I did believe, I wouldn't want her messing with me after death."

"I don't think you much like it before death," I said, smiling.

Jonathan chuckled a little at that. "You're right. I just don't think that she respects anyone or anything. I swear that kind of attitude is what gets people in trouble in horror movies, and I don't care to be the first to be knocked off in the horror movie of Rachel's life."

"Why would you be the first to go?" I asked.

"Well, probably not the first. I'd probably be the second to the last. You know, the pragmatic gay friend who has all the answers, not that she'd listen."

I laughed out loud at that one. "Hopefully we're not in a horror movie because I'm the one who's already creeped out. I thought I heard someone running down the hallway earlier, but no one was there. I have no idea what caused it, but I'd rather not start talking about mysterious paranormal killers."

"I've not heard anything like that," Jonathan said. "I got back to my room kind of late though, so maybe it happened before I was there."

"Maggie found my phone," I said, changing the subject as we rounded the doorway into the hall. It looked dark down the corridor, though the lights were on. The walls seemed just a little too narrow for the length, and I didn't really want to walk down the way.

"I heard that already," Jonathan said. "You have to realize, we're a small group and all there is to do is gossip. I had a late tea with that lovely young woman who's doing the cleaning and she told me."

"There's tea?" I asked.

Jonathan paused at his door. "Oh, come on, now. It's not real tea. I had coffee and a snack. But there's stuff out during a typical British tea time, so that's what I call it."

With that Jonathan gave me a nod and un-locked his door. I hurried to my own door, not caring to be left in the hallway alone. I didn't want to see whatever was making the pounding noises along the hallway.

I thought I heard piano music again but it was fainter than it had been in the afternoon. Perhaps Bethany or Nathan was listening to it, and they were worried about disturbing people in the evening. At any rate, I got my door open without incident.

I locked myself in and started turning on lights. I made sure to have my lantern and the walkie-talkie when I went into the bathroom to shower and change. Tonight I would make sure I had everything on the nightstand before I turned in. I had a lot of research to do, both about the house and the books. I hoped I could get a lot of it done that evening.

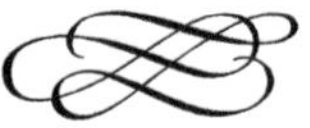

I worked for perhaps an hour without a problem. The internet was slow but not excruciating. I had some low music, a general instrumental that was soft and soothing, playing in the background. I had tried other music but the acoustics of the room made other things echo in strange patterns that knotted my stomach and made my body shiver.

The sheets still smelled clean and slightly of my own personal scents, which told me that while the bed had been tidily made no one had changed out the sheets. There was still the faintest hint of mustiness that pervaded the house, though the chemical lavender smell did its best to push it away. What was it about old houses that made them hold on to their smells? It was like the wood or brick absorbed the scents along with memories.

I'd been reading about the Manor rather than the family this time. I knew I should have been doing some research on the books I had questions on, but I wanted to know about the place. When had it been built and why?

Schilling Manor had been built in the early days of the nineteenth century, not long after Nova Scotia had gotten settled. It had originally been a two-bedroom house made of wood. The Schillings had done well, working in coal, and it was the discovery of a couple of small mines that had led to their riches. I had read much of that already when I'd researched Audra Schilling.

The original manor, which was made up of the central wing, was built between 1830 and 1835. The addition of the east wing was done in the 1880s in two sections, which surprised me. The greenhouse wasn't mentioned, but that could have been built at any time. There were three out-buildings, which housed the staff who didn't live in the main house. Those had, I supposed, fallen into ruin.

The Manor itself was unremarkable architec-turally. Only its size was of any note. Cape Breton wasn't known for its mansions and Schilling Manor was that, copied more after the styles of Old English Aristocracy. The Schillings themselves fancied connections to aristocracy at certain points in their history which, no doubt, had led to the Manor.

Several names that might have been famous in the day, perhaps recognizable to better historians than me, had come to visit at the Manor, both from the United States and England. I found it interesting that few names appeared to be from Scotland, given that Nova Scotia was so heavily settled by Scotsmen.

I searched out the origins of Schilling and found that it was a German name. I wondered how a German had come to Nova Scotia and why. That took me down another rabbit hole of research, but I found nothing to tell me when the Schillings had come across the Atlantic to land in Canada. Even knowing the approximate date that the first house had been built told me nothing.

The lights had dimmed a bit while I worked, although I had done nothing to change anything. It was just that shadows near the corners were longer. I tapped my lamps. I even walked across the room and flicked the lights off and turned them back on, but they stubbornly refused to brighten back to what I had remembered.

The house settled and groaned. Someone flushed a toilet but that familiar sound didn't settle me at all.

I went back to the bed and turned down the

music on my laptop. It suddenly seemed too loud and I didn't want to be noticed there in my bed, which was an odd thing to think of.

The Manor became nearly silent for just a moment. Then, I heard a creak from outside, as if someone were walking down the hallway. More silence, like someone was trying to creep down the hall.

My heart raced.

I shivered, feeling suddenly cold. I drew the covers up around me, sliding down into the bed, not sure if I was doing so to warm up or to hide. The smell of dirt and the damp smell I always associated with moldy books hit me, as if someone had opened a door to a room filled with them.

Nothing in my bedroom had changed.

The knob of the door turned. It should have been locked but it opened all the same, without a squeak. A man walked in.

He was dressed oddly, all in black. I didn't think I recognized him. It was too hard to get a good look at his face to be certain. He walked past me and went to the wardrobe, bending down to look for something. He couldn't have missed me. Did he not care that he was observed?

He stood up from the wardrobe and then walked out of the room. He closed the door carefully behind him. The chill in the room lessened, although the smell remained, a lingering sort of thing.

I slipped out of the bed, going closer to the door. I wasn't sure what I intended to do. Was I going to look out in the hall to call after him? Call him a thief?

I glanced down. The door remained locked.

I froze in place. Had I just seen a ghost?

He'd looked so real, not at all like they make ghosts look in Hollywood, all gauzy and see-through. The man was as real as I was or anyone else I'd seen around the place.

I turned and walked back to the wardrobe and looked inside. I squatted down where he'd been. It was difficult to see in the dim light.

I got up and grabbed the electric lantern which, upon turning it on, threw off a great deal of light, like a beacon.

I walked with it back to the wardrobe and squatted down to look inside once again. I moved a pair of shoes and a backpack I had brought. I felt along the wood, which was smooth. I knocked here and there against the bottom, listening for any different sounds.

One place sounded more hollow than the others.

I started pushing and pulling in that area, trying to see if there was something that would open. I pushed down hard, thinking perhaps it was a spring. I ran my fingers over the wood searching for any sort of indent, like a lever, but nothing. I ran my hands up the wall to see if there was a lever there, but I could find nothing.

I all but crawled into the space holding the light high to see what I could. There was the slightest difference in the wood in that small area, like someone had replaced it as some point.

I began to try to slide the wood one way or another. Nothing.

I kept at it, knowing that something had to work. I was nearly positive there was a hidden compartment there. I just didn't know how to get to it.

I was tempted to see if I had something heavy that would work as a hammer to break through the wood, but I wasn't quite ready to destroy the wardrobe bottom just yet.

In frustration I must have pushed down at just the correct angle because I felt the board move backwards, just a little. I tried again. It took some doing, but I finally got the little door to open.

I looked inside. There was an old, perhaps ancient, pressed flower. I avoided touching it, lest it disintegrate. There was also a pile of what appeared to be letters tied with a ribbon that had once been red, but was now a pale pinkish color that I couldn't imagine anyone choosing.

I carefully picked out the letters and took them

to the bed. The find had so excited me I had forgotten to be frightened. My heart wasn't racing.
Instead, I felt rather giddy, as if I had won a prize.
I couldn't wait to read the letters and perhaps find
out who my ghostly visitor had been.

CHAPTER 12

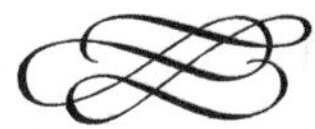

Trying to read the letters kept me up far too late, and when I woke up to the loud buzzing alarm, I noticed that I was curled around them on the bed with all the lights still on. I was rather horrified with myself for treating the old paper that way.

Fortunately, the paper was probably less than a hundred years old. The scent of rose still wafted faintly from it. My best guess was that they were letters between Audra Schilling and her young man. They weren't signed, although one person used the initial A. The other used only an XO, which I assumed was for hugs and kisses.

If Audra's father hadn't liked the match, certainly it would have been smart of them to not sign the letters. She could get away with the initial.

After all, her father could guess they were from her, or from her mother, but the handwriting was likely to give her away anyway. The young man, though, had far more to lose.

I'd started deciphering them and found that I was reading backwards in the pile, so I had turned it over and begun to read a second time. I had gotten through only two of the letters in that direction before sleep had claimed me.

Audra had sent the first letter asking all sorts of questions about the war and hoping that his— whoever *he* was—health would be okay. Oddly she hadn't used his name anywhere, though she asked many questions about what might have made him feel better.

His reply was that he didn't have the words to describe the horrors of war or his injuries but that he would be willing to discuss things with her in person next time he was at the Manor. He went on to talk about how lucky he felt that he worked in a place where the mistress cared so much about the people who worked for them.

He didn't sign his name in his letter either. It made me suspicious, and I wondered if something had gone on between them even before the war. Perhaps there were clues in Audra's first letter to something that had gone on earlier. After all, the initial correspondence appeared quite innocent to outsider's eyes, and the only issue was the lack of the young man's name.

Like an old woman, the early morning Manor creaked and groaned. Light came through the split from the curtains that covered the windows. I looked out, pressing my nose against the cool glass. The sky was blue and clear. I doubted there would be fog or rain that day, although being from the south, I knew you could never really be certain when it would rain. The weather could change by afternoon.

I was nearly dressed when I heard the soft closing of a door not far away. I wondered if it were Nathan or Jonathan who had left. I finished quickly, grabbing my key and my walkie-talkie. Just as I put my hand out to the knob, a door slammed nearby, making me jump.

I opened my own door and wasn't surprised to see Rachel hurrying by. She didn't give me a second glance. I left more slowly, making sure my own door didn't slam and then locked it.

I had put the letters in a drawer with my purse so no one would disturb them. I knew I ought to tell Bethany and Nathan about them, but I didn't want them taken from me before I read them all. I had no idea why. I suppose it was because I had seen a man dressed all in black placing them in the floor of a wardrobe where I'd found them.

The dining hall smelled of eggs and bacon,

and I saw that Pat and Bob had put out warming trays with poached eggs and Canadian bacon. There were English muffins to toast and even a small gravy boat filled with Hollandaise sauce for those who wished it. I put together my Eggs Benedict sans the Hollandaise, which I've never liked. I added a couple of slices of the tomatoes that were on a separate plate. I took that back to my place before grabbing my mug for coffee.

Nathan and Jonathan both greeted me. Rachel ignored me as she came back to the table with her own mug but no food.

As I sat, she got up and went to the sideboard.

"How was your night?" Nathan asked.

"It was fine. I didn't get as much research done as I'd hoped," I said. "How about yours?"

Nathan nodded.

"I can't imagine doing research upstairs. I have a computer in the room they gave me as an office and half the time that's excruciating," Jonathan said.

"We've done everything we could," Nathan told him.

Jonathan waved him off. He had a full plate of eggs and Hollandaise. No tomatoes for him though. "I know. I just don't have Lara's patience, I guess."

Nathan smiled. "You did when you first got here."

Jonathan nodded, thinking about that. How quickly things had changed for him. He seemed very settled in already and still seemed enthusiastic.

"The power stayed on, which was good," I said.

Nathan and Jonathan both chuckled. Rachel came with her plate of food, just an English muffin, tomatoes and some fruit that I'd managed to miss.

"I hate when they do eggs," Rachel grumbled.

"You hate that they won't let you cook according to your daily diet," Jonathan said. "It'd be easier if you picked one and stuck to it."

Rachel glared at him and dug into the food she had.

"The day looks like it'll be pretty," I said, changing the subject. The eggs were perfectly done, not always easy to achieve with poached.

"If you get an opportunity, today would be the perfect day to follow the path to the bluff," Nathan said. "Perhaps when you need a break in the afternoon. It's not a long walk."

Jonathan had a lot to say about the view and the ability of painters to capture it. Rachel was silent.

I finished my breakfast and settled back with my coffee. I hadn't slept any more the last night than I had the night before, but I felt more awake.

Perhaps because this last night my sleeplessness had been more by choice. That didn't mean I could keep my eyes open without a good infusion of caffeine.

"Do they have sodas around for the afternoon?" I asked. "If not, can I ask for some?"

"Pepsi in the fridge," Nathan said. "You can just go grab one or ask Pat."

If it came in a bottle with a top, I could even feel okay about taking it with me over to the library. That would go a long way to keeping my mind fresh while I worked on the books.

Jonathan excused himself and went out to make his way to his work area. Rachel got up to get seconds of her breakfast. Nathan was still sipping his coffee. His silence didn't feel uncomfortable, just the silence of a man who had nothing else to say.

I finished my coffee before he finished his. I hadn't brought down my notes from the night before, so after saying goodbye I went back up to my room. I grabbed my notes, noting absently that whoever Maggie had hired to clean hadn't gotten to my room just yet, not that I was expecting it or complaining. It was merely something I noticed.

I locked the door behind me, pocketed my key, and considered which way to go. The hallway here had to run into the main hallway in the center wing. I decided to follow the corridor in that direction rather than taking the stairs.

In the back of my mind, I recalled that Nathan and Maggie had both said it was better to have someone with you when you were walking through the Manor, but surely there were enough people working. I heard distant hammering that sounded like it came from above.

I passed four more doors on either side of the hallway. The lights became dimmer. I looked back and noticed that the lights were only on to the end of those three doors but the hallway continued on. I continued walking. It wasn't like I was suddenly going to be lost in the dark.

The musty smell got stronger. Then I began to smell an old-fashioned floral scent. It reminded me of sachets I had fingered at an antique show. I wondered where it came from as I continued down the hall, which still ran straight, though I didn't understand how it could be so long. It was darker than ever.

I kept going. Although I was feeling cooler, I wasn't freezing as if I had encountered a ghost. The floors looked darker and shinier. I wondered if they'd been refinished already.

The wallpaper also seemed to have more color. There were red roses and sprigs of lavender and rosemary on the paper that ran above the chair rail. I paused, pressing my nose closer to the paper, looking for a scent of fresh glue, but there was nothing. Perhaps this part of the hallway was always in shadow so the paper hadn't had a chance to fade.

There was still no turn and I started to feel uncomfortable. There was something wrong.

I heard a bell ring in the distance, like an old-fashioned dinner bell. I turned back the way I had come. The hallway seemed to stretch into infinity. I had had nightmares of this sort when I was going through school. Hallways that never ended or running towards something only to have it move ever further away. Had I fallen asleep in my room and I was dreaming?

I walked quickly back the way I had come, wondering what was going on.

"Don't do it, Miss," a woman's voice said behind a door that I noticed was slightly ajar. There was even a trace of light coming out.

I wondered if she was talking to me. I paused, not going any closer.

"Don't be silly, Marybeth. It's just a letter."

"Your father…" The speaker, who had to be Marybeth, trailed off.

I sucked in a breath. Was I hearing ghosts now? I crept closer to the door, wanting to look in, afraid of what I might see.

When I peeked in, the room was empty. I stepped back.

The floral scent was gone. I was left with the chemical smell that held a trace of lavender.

The floor creaked. I jumped and turned.

Nathan was standing in the hallway.

"Were you looking for me?" he asked.

"What?" I turned and glanced around. I was standing outside the room I had been assigned, facing the door to Nathan's room. If he'd come up a bit earlier, he might have seen me trying to peer through a crack into his room, although, now that I looked, the door was shut tightly.

"I think I may have had a moment where the Manor seemed to turn me around," I said shakily.

Nathan nodded but looked at me strangely. He paused to let me step away from his door and go to his room.

I was still shaking my head.

"Do you need to lie down?" he asked. The strange look had been replaced by one of concern.

"I think I'm fine," I said. "Thank you. I'll just go to the library by way of the stairs."

Nathan nodded. "This corridor doesn't link up with the main corridor in the Center Wing. There's an upstairs drawing room that separates the two wings, so you have to go downstairs and around or up to the third floor, but there's so much construction up there, I'd recommend down."

"It is a strange house," I said.

"Poorly planned, I'd say." Nathan laughed. "I hope if I ever get rich enough to build a mansion I have the sense to design it a little better."

I smiled and turned to leave. I wanted to be alone even if I didn't really want to be alone. What I really wanted was to call Tessie and leave the Manor. A hotel room in Halifax sounded great. I wasn't sure Sydney would be far enough way. The problem was if I left, I might not ever come back.

The stairs down to the kitchen were normal. The dining hall was normal. Rachel was still there eating. I exited the far door and walked down that corridor to the library. The lighting stayed the same, the floors creaked in a normal and consistent fashion compared to yesterday. No strange voices accosted me. No strange moments of cold.

I breathed in and tried to calm my heart rate. Unfortunately, neither my heart nor my mind had any intention of being calmed. There was too much to take in.

The lights were burning in the library when I got there. I immediately went to the computer and sat down. I had my pile of books which I needed to finish. I'd work until I got through the section I'd begun and then do some research online.

It was easy to get lost in the work. I love books, all books. And these were just modern enough that I began to recognize authors. There was work by Dostoyevsky and Thomas Hardy. Neither was in particularly good condition, but they were both likely be worth something. I'd need to research a little more.

By the time I'd finished the section, it was past noon. I was calmer. Nothing had happened, although even with the mask I'd found in one of the office supply boxes I had sneezed a few times given the amount of dust in the air. Such were the problems of old books.

I stood, making sure I had the walkie-talkie, and started down towards the dining hall. I'd wash in the funny little powder room around the corner from the kitchen.

I felt a sudden chill when I passed by the main front doors. I glanced over, wondering if one of them were open, but they were closed tight. I even noticed new locks on them, shiny against the dullness and dust of so much of the rest of the place.

Still, it was cold. I hurried away down the hallway, shadows falling around like several large dogs I might take for a walk on a leash. I looked around for what might be making those shadows but saw nothing. The house was unusually silent.

This was worse than the usual sounds. My heart started to race again.

I heard a footfall behind me, loud in the silence.

I turned but there was no one there.

I felt in my pocket for the walkie-talkie, glad to find the smooth plastic still there, in case I needed it.

I walked quickly, my shoes squeaking loudly against the too-silent floor.

No other footfalls pursued me.

The dining hall was empty, but I smelled food, both the fresher smells of tomato, probably a soup, and less fresh smells of bacon, probably from this morning. At least that was a normal thing.

I hurried towards the kitchen, glancing at the sideboard, glad to see there was plenty of fresh lunch meat and bread as well as soup.

A pot clanged against the counter in the kitchen. Pat and Bob were working as usual, murmuring to each other about getting something prepared for dinner. I gave them a smile and a wave before going into the bathroom to wash.

My face was pale in the mirror, my eyes looking haunted. Of course, that would be normal for someone who was being haunted, wouldn't it?

CHAPTER 13

Back in the library, I lost myself in the work. Each book was a new challenge and a new puzzle. While most were musty, there were three shelves of books that all smelled faintly of citrus. They didn't appear to be books owned by women, so I could only conclude that whoever had owned them was a lover of oranges. One of them was an early graphic medical text.

I looked through it, the pages making a soft sound as I turned them, a pleasant counterpoint to the louder groans and creaks of the house. The pictures I found were detailed but often quite inaccurate. The medical knowledge there would have been amusing if I wasn't certain that this was a book people had relied on for healthcare information.

Wound cleaning relied on alcohol that would also be used for drink. There was no mention of washing hands or cleaning a wound. I didn't know if the herbs mentioned would be helpful or not, but there were some graphic descriptions of gangrene that I didn't care to read about.

Other books were more pleasant. There were a couple on political philosophy. One on plants. They were all just piled together. While they weren't exactly grouped by year, those that were out of place were usually only a few years older than the others. I began to think that these books had been kept in order of purchase. That would have been fine in a small library, but in one this size? I had no idea how anyone had ever found anything.

I continued with my cataloging, looking at each book to see if any of them were obviously moldy. Those would get sequestered to try and keep the mold from spreading, though I suspected once I found any mold, the entire shelf, if not the whole section, was likely to be done for. So far things had looked pretty good, which was a surprise given everything else I'd found.

I got so engrossed in my work that I was surprised to note when it was nearly five in the afternoon. The sun was lower in the sky, hitting at such an angle as to bathe the whole room in a flickering orange glow. I felt as if I were in a burning house, and my heart leapt a bit when I first noticed it. Fortunately, I was getting used to such shocks and quickly calmed myself.

I decided to pause and see if I could contact Tessie. I had emailed her and hadn't received anything back. Skype was installed on the system and I tried giving her a ring, although there was no answer. I also got a warning that the video wasn't clear. Finally as I was about to hang up, I also got a warning that my sound wasn't very good either.

I rung off, hoping she'd notice and perhaps worry about me a little bit. I sent her another note to remind her my phone may not be working very well and to ask if we could set up a time where I could talk to her via the computer. I suggested Saturday or Sunday when I could feel okay about taking some time off and chatting. If nothing else, I could drive into town and use my cell phone. Sydney would have to have cell phone service.

I put a few books back on the shelves. My hand brushed against the edge of one of the sections and it felt rough. I rubbed at it a little and a piece of wood shifted, leaving a small opening, which didn't look like a naturally rotted spot in the upright piece of lumber.

I left the books, bringing over the electric lantern. The opening was probably too small to hold a rat, but if there were large spiders in there, I had no desire to touch one.

I shone the lantern in there. The spiders in the alcove were long dead, only stray dark parts left on webs that were old and frail. A small book sat in there but I couldn't read a title from that angle.

I walked back to the desk moving quickly around the low bookshelves that separated me from the wall. I searched through the drawers, thankful to find a ruler. I used that to brush away the webs and to pull the book out of its alcove. Having made sure nothing was on the back of the book, I lifted it carefully, dusting it off. I put a post it on the section and then filled the books back in.

I walked to the desk, taking this book with me. It was small and thin. When I opened it—carefully, not knowing how well preserved it was—I realized that it was a bankbook. But why would it be hidden in such a small place? And how had it gotten left there? Did Bethany know about it? Perhaps she had even more of an inheritance than she thought.

I wanted to rush it to her and then go to the bank that had issued it to see what fortune was there now. Naturally, it wasn't my place to do such a thing.

I was hesitant to take the book out of the library. The change in temperature wouldn't be good for it, though its only value would be if there was money in the account left behind. Still, once you start archiving, it's hard to break that habit, so

I hesitated while I pondered what was best for the book.

I didn't like the idea of leaving it in the library either. Surely it had been hidden for a reason. I thought of my phone going missing. Was that thief looking for a bankbook? What if Bethany wasn't the only heir?

I told myself I'd read too many mysteries. I put the little book in the bottom drawer of the desk and pushed it towards the back, so it wasn't easily seen. Then I put a bunch of the index cards I used to make notes on in the front of the drawer. It would hide the book without really touching it or covering it up. I'd mention it to Bethany when I got her alone.

I closed the drawer, still thinking. I shut off the computer, listening as it powered down. The house settled around me, sounds that I was beginning to get used to. Then I went back through the dining hall, intending to go to my room and wash up. I wasn't late for dinner this time.

Back upstairs I heard someone playing the piano again. Once again, it was silenced when I closed my door. It had to be someone across the hall, I thought. After all, I should be able to hear it otherwise. I could hear doors slamming and people walking down the hall. Tonight I even heard something heavy fall on the floor above me.

I didn't jump despite the unexpected thud

right above my head. I must have been getting used to things in Schilling Manor.

I took off my sweater and washed up in the bathroom. I had enough time to change my shirt. I hated to put the sweater back on. It needed a good wash but I had nothing else that would easily hold the walkie-talkie in a pocket. I searched through my things and came up with an oversized shirt that had a large pocket on the breast. I looked silly carrying the walk-talkie there but I could hold on to it, maybe, and then just use the pocket if I had to.

I decided to do that. I'd also have to ask someone about laundry. Did someone do it for us or was there a coin operated machine someplace?

I picked up my phone, looking for any messages. I had a call from my mom and one from Tessie. I also had one from a friend at work. There was one voicemail which I was pretty sure was from Mom. I tried listen to it but I had no bars. I moved closer to the window to try and retrieve it and that helped.

I could hear Mom's message, just.

I had a couple of texts as well, and as I stood near the window three more came in. One was from Tessie, saying that it sounded like I was pretty cut off from everything.

I sighed and plugged the phone back in, although I wasn't sure why I was doing so. It wasn't like I'd used any power. It made me wonder how I was supposed to charge the walkie-talkies.

Another thing to ask when I went down to dinner.

I decided I'd go down, even if I was a little early. I could have some coffee while I waited. Not that I really needed more caffeine, but I was feeling out of sorts. I wanted to talk to Bethany but wasn't sure where to find her in the Manor or how to set up a time to talk. I was going to have find out where and how people scheduled these meetings too, rather than just hoping to run into someone at a meal.

I picked up my key and the walkie talkie and then headed down the hall to the stairs. Jonathan came out of his room as I passed by. I paused to wait for him.

"Early tonight, then," Jonathan said. "Usually you come straight from the library."

"I worried if I started a new shelf I'd get lost and forget the time," I said. "So I came up and got changed."

Jonathan nodded. "I do that all the time. I missed dinner once and didn't notice until it was getting dark. I had to call out for help on the walkie-talkie. Everyone left the table to come find me. It seemed like forever before they did. I was lucky I always carried a lantern with me because it was dark where I was."

"It's weird that you get lost in this place. I almost did this afternoon just in this hallway. It was like it changed."

"I try to remind myself that the kids in Harry Potter didn't find the changing stairs in Hogwarts scary, but this place gives me the creeps. I'm probably just going crazy or something. Maybe there's some toxic mold."

We were halfway down the stairs when he said that. "Do you suppose?" I asked. Wasn't that what they blamed the witch hunt in Salem on? Could there be any truth?

"I've no idea," Jonathan said. "But it makes far more sense than the house moving hallways and corridors randomly, don't you think?"

He was right about that. We turned towards the kitchen, waving at Pat and Bob who returned the greetings. I asked Jonathan about laundry. He said I just had to leave it out and marked for the people who cleaned the room every day.

"I do mine every Friday, so they're busy then. I have no idea how careful they are about keeping things separated. I'd hate to find your bras in with my shirts."

Jonathan had a way of making me laugh. We both got water from the pitchers that had already been set out. Jonathan breathed deeply. I didn't smell much so I wondered what was on the menu.

"Low smells for dinner means they can make

it fast. Probably a stir fry. We'll have a choice to add meat or not," Jonathan said. "No salad probably because they figure there are plenty of vegetables in the stir fry. After, they usually make some sort of baked or fried apple. I think it's the closest to baking those two get, and honestly, those apples are heavenly!"

It sounded good and different from our other meals. I was looking forward to it. Given that Nova Scotia relied so heavily on seafood I was surprised we hadn't gotten more, something I mentioned to Jonathan.

"Seafood here is always fresh. It's hard when you live so far out. We may get most of the food fresh because we can't count on the electricity, but it's hard to plan for varying numbers of people with seafood."

It sort of made sense.

We chatted about small things while we waited and sipped our water with lemon.

Nathan came in with Bethany and the two waved at us.

"So how is everything going?" Bethany asked.

"I found something I wanted to show you," I said. "I was wondering if we could meet sometime tomorrow."

"Book questions should go to Nathan," Bethany said.

"I'm not sure it's a book. I found it hidden in a

small compartment," I told her. "I think it is something you ought to see."

Bethany gave Nathan a look then said, "We'll both come down to the library about nine or so, right after breakfast. You can show us then. But really this sort of thing should go through Nathan."

Nathan nodded. "It does sound unusual, so chances are I'd want to show you anyway."

Bethany gave him a look that said they'd discuss that later.

I tried to remember what had been said before. Bethany had been sweet and smiling and assuring me that I could come to her with any questions. Clearly any questions meant general things that she could talk to me about and not specific questions about the collection. Or else she worried that people would be taking up too much of her time. I wondered exactly what it was she did while the rest of us were pawing through her inheritance trying to put specific valuations on it.

CHAPTER 14

The next morning, after a dinner of stir fry —which was tasty—and conversation— which was interesting, if mundane—and then an evening of reading the letters as best I could, I woke feeling more refreshed than I had in several days. I hadn't been kept up by ghosts nor by power outages that made me think of ghosts. I washed with the lightly scented soap I'd brought along, a familiar spicy scent, and was finally re- laxed enough to enjoy it.

I hadn't learned anything much from the let- ters the evening before. They were just letters be- tween two people who increasingly seemed to be in love with each other. A few were short letters, asking to meet "in their place" which could have been anywhere, though I felt I could narrow it down to someplace outside on the grounds. I also came to learn, over the course of reading, that the mysterious beau was likely some sort of stone mason. It wasn't much of a lead but it was as much as I could find.

I would look to see if I could find any ledgers in the library and see if I could match a name to the beau. I remembered Jonathan's story, and that gave me other bits and pieces I could patch together to get a better picture of the couple.

I heard a door close softly across the way when I was nearly dressed to start work. I paused to leave my dirty clothes in a pile on the chair with a note for the cleaning person. I'd love to have my sweater back. The house was so dusty that even my oversized shirt was beginning to feel faintly gritty and I'd only worn that once. I left my room and started down the hallway.

Bethany was just coming out of her room.

"Good morning!" She was bright and cheery even before coffee. I wasn't sure I could take it.

"Good morning," I said, thankful that I wasn't as worn out this morning as I had been the other two days.

"I wanted to tell you that I appreciate you coming to me about something that you found," Bethany said. "Nathan hates it when his workers go directly to me, though. He's a wonderful coordinator but he can be a bit fussy."

She had waited until we were safely in the kitchen before mentioning that. Bob and Pat weren't paying us any attention. I smelled bacon, eggs, and cheese and wondered what wonderful things they'd made for us that morning.

"I had no idea," I said. "It was just that it seemed more personal than something from a library which is why I wanted to talk to you."

The dining room was quiet when we passed through the entry to it. Only Jonathan sat at the table, but he appeared lost in through, sipping at his mug of coffee. The smell of coffee and bacon made my mouth water.

"I understand," Bethany said. "And I don't mind, really. In fact, I keep an office on the other side of the kitchen. It's not terribly quiet with Bob and Pat and the pots and pans all day, plus you hear the bell from the side door, which is what everyone uses, but I get halfway decent phone reception if I'm by the window. And there's a set of French doors to the outside if I need to go out there and talk!"

So she did have an office. I had imagined her upstairs near the main bedrooms, but I suppose it worked well to have an office near the kitchen.

"Ah, frittatas this morning," Bethany breathed

in, walking quickly over to the sideboard. "My favorite."

I grabbed my mug and got coffee first. Then I joined her at the sideboard. She was toasting an English muffin to go with her frittata. I added some of the fruit to my plate. There were muffins but I wasn't that interested in those just then.

I settled in to start eating. Jonathan had a plate that was mostly empty but for a few crumbs and a bread plate that held a muffin that was still waiting to be eaten.

He smiled and nodded and soon enough we were all chatting away about food and the weather and general topics that are always safe to discuss among workers.

It wasn't long before I was down to just my coffee, the mug wonderfully warm in my hands. The dining hall was one of the warmer rooms in the Manor, at least in June. I wondered if that would continue to be true when July and August came. I had looked it up so I knew that Nova Scotia could get fairly warm and quite humid during the late summer. As far as I could tell there was no air conditioning, which meant the place might be rather stifling later on, but for now it was comfortable to cool.

Cold, if you counted the freezing spots that moved around like the wandering phantom they just might be harbingers of.

I finished my coffee and headed to the library. Bethany didn't follow me. I wondered if she'd wait for Nathan, who, unusually, still wasn't at breakfast.

I entered the large room. The lights were on, but they looked dim. There was light streaming through the windowpanes, but it didn't seem to reach as far into the room as it should have. I heard a squeak and then something dropped. I turned quickly, straining to see what was going on.

A shadow moved towards me. I waited for the chill to come, my heart pattering like a scampering kitten. I wondered if this was the same ghost who had visited me in my room the other night or if the Manor had more than one. I shuddered at the thought.

It was a silly fear, really. The ghost in the room had done nothing but show me the place where letters were hidden. Still, ghosts were dead people. You weren't supposed to see dead people.

Granted, I think I saw my grandfather the day he died, sitting in the chair in the living room. He'd held out his arms to me. Before I'd gone running to him, I'd called out excitedly to my mother that Grandpa was there. I'd leaped onto the chair to find it was only a chair.

I was so disappointed. My mom was angry with me because she was on the phone with my grandmother learning that Grandpa had just died.

To this day, I am certain I saw him in that chair. There was no way I could have known what they were talking about.

While that hadn't been a scary moment, either, that was someone who had loved me and brought me joy. I didn't know these people. I didn't know their reasons for being around.

The shadow took form and when it was past the last of the low bookshelves, I saw that it was only Nathan.

"There you are," he said. "I wanted to be sure I was on time for our meeting."

I didn't have a watch but I had figured that if Bethany were still at breakfast I'd have plenty of time. I knew that I'd been down in the dining hall well before eight and it was unlikely that I'd spent over an hour making idle chitchat while I ate.

"I'm sure you aren't," I said, walking into the room.

It was cool but not the freezing chill that I experienced with otherworldly sensations. I walked through the room, glancing from side to side but nothing seem to be moved. I thought some of the books on the desk had been rearranged. The center drawer wasn't quite closed. I didn't immediately go to the bottom drawer because, for some reason, I suddenly didn't quite trust Nathan.

"I don't think you are, either," Nathan said.

"But I did want to go over some procedures before Bethany came in."

I worried a little that he would chastise me for talking to her rather than just talking to him, but instead he talked about a number of little things that hadn't been gone over. While he talked about his office, a room that was in the wing we were housed in, on the other side of the stairwell, he also had plenty of questions for me about the software.

It quickly became clear that he had no idea what they had purchased for me, and I showed him how I was inputting information and where he could find my notes. I even made up an account for him. What I didn't tell him was that he didn't have complete access to the database. I did make an account for Bethany as well and gave her full acccss. After all, she was the one paying me.

It was frustrating to think that I had such reservations about Nathan. I hated to voice them to anyone. No one had said a bad word about him, except possibly Rachel, and she said nasty things about everyone. She was another person who wasn't at breakfast, which surprised me. I hoped she was okay. She'd been unusually quiet at dinner.

As I was finishing up showing Nathan how to use the software, Bethany came in. "I'm early, I know, but if we're all here, I can't wait to see what you've found."

Relief flooded through me, although a different anxiety began in my belly. What if Nathan had found that book and taken it out of the desk for his own purposes? How would that look? And what would I say if that happened?

CHAPTER 15

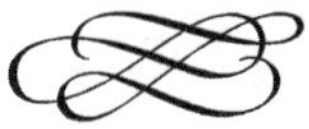

I opened the drawer, listening to the shush of the wood rubbing against wood as I pulled it out. The slide wasn't quite smooth and there was a clunk as the drawer hit one side. My index cards were still there, falling this way and that. I didn't think I'd put that many cards in the drawer the night before. Did they looked a little messier than they had been when I'd left? I couldn't be certain.

I reached into the back. My heart sank when my hand felt nothing but the wooden bottom.

My fingers explored the wood, searching for paper.

I found something. Larger than an index card.

A small book.

I couldn't keep the smile off my face.

The room rushed back, with its too musty, dusty smell and the creaks and clanks of the house as the heating sputtered and the building settled or whatever it was that it did. It made too much noise too often to actually be a house settling.

"Here it is," I said, bringing the book out. The cover was dark and almost black, though I'd cleaned off what I could. The name was faded and almost impossible to read, though if you looked closely you could make out the name of a large Canadian bank.

Had it been anything other than a bankbook, I'd have set it aside for more cleaning, though I wasn't set up to do a full cleaning of damaged books. Those would need to be sent out. It was one of the things Nathan and I had talked about earlier.

There was a monastery that did book restoration work and Bethany had a contract with them. I would box up the books that needed the most work and then we'd send them off to the Monks. Nathan had given me a website link so that I could look up their particular requests for various types of damage, including what to do if the books were water damaged.

I handed the bankbook to Bethany.

She took it carefully, almost hesitant to open it.

She set the book on the desk and carefully pushed back the cover, showing the first page.

There was a man's name in the book but I hadn't recognized it. Schilling Coal was also named as a co-owner of the account. That I did recognize.

"I've never seen this," Bethany said. She reached to turn a page and then looked at me as if she'd made a serious error.

"So long as your hands are clean, it's fine," I said. "Even if they're a little dusty, the value of this is in the information about the account. I would think it would have been part of Audra's will unless she didn't know about the account at all."

"It's for Schilling Coal but the other name wasn't my great-grandfather's," Bethany said. "I'd heard about the Hannas, of course, but I never believed…"

I waited for her to continue. If I looked at the name just right, it did look like someone had written Robert Hanna on the bankbook. I had no idea who that was.

Nathan said nothing. He was sitting back, face carefully neutral. I had a feeling he had an opinion about what I'd found but didn't care to say anything in front of either me or Bethany. I wasn't sure which of us he wished to keep that hidden from, but I suspected it was me. Or per-haps both of us.

Bethany looked up, seeing the question in my eyes.

"Another inglorious chapter in the Schilling family history," Bethany said. "It was rumored that my great-grandfather helped Robert Hanna with shipping during prohibition. At one point, I guess Hanna didn't pay him for something and it devolved into a sort of feud. I'm not certain of the details. A few months later, Hanna was bankrupt and he ended up throwing himself into the ocean, or so I've heard. This bankbook suggests the stories might have been true."

"The names on the book suggests the business they were in was legitimate," Nathan said. "It involved Schilling Coal, not your great-grandfather."

"Or not," Bethany said. "It's hard to say what it was for. I'll have to call the bank and see what they can tell me. If Robert Hanna had heirs and they're still around, this might belong as much to them as it does to me. My attorney may end up having to solve this particular mystery."

"I thought Hanna's son Eddie was killed in the war," Nathan said.

"He was," Bethany said. "Audra talked about it all the time. I guess she had quite a crush on him, probably because her father so disapproved."

I wondered if Eddie Hanna was the writer of the letters to Audra Schilling. It would make sense in a way. It would have been particularly heartbreaking if there had been a falling out between the two families. Of course, would Eddie have been allowed on the property if the falling out had been bad enough that Robert Hanna was killed over it?

"Where exactly did you find this?" Nathan asked.

I got up and took the two of them across the library. I think only *my* shoes squeaked. I was going to have to see what Bethany was wearing that allowed her to walk so quietly across the floors here. I found the sticky note I had left up and moved the books there, pointing out the tiny cubby.

"I just rubbed a rough spot on the wood and it came off," I said. "It was probably a little secret door but was worn down by the years."

"How ingenious!" Bethany said. She clapped her hands. "I always hoped there were secret cubbyholes around or maybe even a secret room. Aunt Audra never really let me go running around to play, not that I wanted to. When she was alive, it was just her and a few servants and the place was far too gloomy to go searching for secret passages. If I found one, I was afraid a ghost would pop out at me!"

I didn't want to tell her that ghosts had already popped out at me. Nor did I care to share that I'd found two such cubbies in as many days. How many more would I find? Of course, I'd had help from the ghosts that she said she feared.

"How did you say you found it?" Nathan asked, giving me a long look, as if he suspected me of something.

"I think I was rubbing the edge of the section. It felt odd. The wood just sort of pulled off. I used a ruler to make sure there weren't any bugs on it and pulled it out," I explained. I rubbed the shelf and sure enough, I found the thin piece of wood that had covered the cubby.

I'm not certain Nathan was convinced, and he had a look on his face that suggested he wanted to say more.

Bethany, however, interrupted and said, "This is just fantastic! Imagine if we clean that up, maybe put the little door back on and let everyone know there are hidden panels. They'll go looking for it. I could hide a small prize inside. People would love hunting for it!"

I could imagine that people in general would love the hunt. I wasn't sure about artists. Weren't they coming on a retreat to do artwork? I couldn't figure out how hunting for a hidden cubby would help them with their creativity, but then again, I wasn't planning an artist's retreat.

Nathan shrugged and said that he had to get going.

"I'll let you know what the bankers say,"

Bethany said. She didn't appear all that excited about an increase in her inheritance, nor did she seem worried about losing it. It was just that I'd found a piece of her history that seemed exciting to her. Which was interesting considering how cagy Jonathan had been about talking about Bethany's family. I wondered why that was.

CHAPTER 16

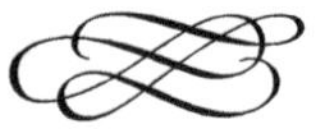

When Bethany and Nathan were gone, I sat at the desk for a few minutes, thinking. I wanted to scribble down what I'd learned but I didn't trust paper because someone could be going through my things. I didn't trust this computer because it wasn't just mine. I opened the other drawers until I found the one holding the notecards. I made a couple of notes that would mean nothing to anyone else and slipped the card into my pocket.

I drew in a breath and found the mask that I'd been wearing. It smelled of dust and coffee, probably because I'd been breathing on it. Then I got up, listening to the creak of the chair, wondered briefly if anything in this house didn't creak, and started on a new shelf of books.

I buried myself in cataloging, working my way quickly through the books. I found one book that had what appeared to be the start of mold, so I set that aside. I'd look up how to pack it later on. I spent a bit of time examining the shelf it sat on and paying closer attention to the other books. There were a few spots that might be mold, and I tried to pull out the shelf but it wouldn't budge.

Later, I thought, I'd ask Nathan who I should talk to about the shelf. It was only one book and in the early stages, but something was going to need to be replaced and I wouldn't feel good until the whole area had been taken out or at least painted over with a mold killing paint. Better safe than sorry.

Of course, I thought, the books really needed to be in an environmentally controlled room but that wasn't going to happen in this old Manor. The most valuable of them would no doubt be sent away to a university where they could be kept in appropriate conditions.

I really wanted to wash my hands again. Keeping them clean working with the old books was a nearly impossible task. Even gloves would be dusty and useless in no time.

I went back to cataloging the next shelf and continued to work my way through the section. Every time I thought I had gotten a bit of work done, I'd look back at what I still had to do, just in this room, and feel as if this was a never-ending task. I sighed.

The next book had a note in it. "To Marie, with love, Robert." It made me think of Robert Hanna and I wondered if this was indeed one of his books or if it had belonged to a different Robert, perhaps one of the Schillings. I made a note about the inscription. Perhaps I would ask Bethany about a family tree. It would be nice to be able to understand who the inscription was speaking about.

It would also help me while I tried to figure out the mysterious ghosts that seemed to plague the Manor. She was the obvious source of information. I could try Nathan but I doubted he'd know who these people were.

I gathered a new section of books. These were less impressive and there was almost an order to them. Everything in that section was on economic theory. It was old economic theory to be sure, most of the books coming from around the turn of the twentieth century, but all were on the same subject. Either the reader was a real fan of economics and I'd be buried in it for the next several shelves, or someone had actually tried to put the books in order.

I hoped for the latter. Economics are not all that interesting no matter what era people are talking about.

However, once I got going on the cataloging, it made things move quickly and I was through two more shelves in record time. None of the books appeared to be particularly valuable. They were in good but not excellent condition, even for their age. No mold, thankfully.

Two more shelves later and I moved from economics to ancient history. A much more fascinating subject, and it appeared that the family felt that way, too. Many of these books were missing pages. A few had notes taken in the margins. I wondered who had studied the subject.

This was why books fascinated me. They held their own histories. Who handled them and who read them? Who made those notes? The handwriting was like a ghostly memory of someone else using the book. Those were the types of ghosts I liked.

One of the books smelled like oranges and I found a small section of what I thought might be fossilized orange peel stuck between two pages. It had blackened over the years and the citrus had bled through into other pages, discoloring them and making much of the book unreadable. I doubted that one could be salvaged, and I put it in its own special pile. I wondered if I should go back and look at the books on the earlier shelves that had smelled of citrus. Perhaps the handler had been this same orange lover, though I hadn't found any evidence of orange peels in those books.

I was reminded of the librarian who once told me she had found a strip of bacon in a book in the book drop. At least this wasn't that bad. Bacon would surely have called rats.

It was impressive that there were no rats even with the citrus, although perhaps rats weren't overly fond of citrus. I moved along. In another book I found a pressed lily. I set that aside. I would need a small box for finds like that. Also for any letters that might have been stuck in a book and forgotten about.

I put back the last stack of books and decided to head off to lunch. I could ask Pat or Bob about a box. Surely they would have them in the kitchen.

I picked up my walkie-talkie and left the library. I hurried through the entry, past the stairs. I heard several thumps up above and I wondered what the contractors were working on today. They seemed closer than usual.

The hallway to the dining room was darker than I remembered. And colder, although I tried to tell myself that it wasn't the freezing chill that I'd been experiencing when something odd happened. I smelled basil and thyme, perhaps a hint of rosemary. I wondered what Pat and Bob were making for lunch.

I turned into the dining hall and immediately realized something was wrong. The hall was lit by flickering candles and the table was set for dozens. A bunch of servants dressed in costumes that hadn't been worn for over a hundred years were arranging flowers. Everything looked so real. There were no shimmers. I thought for a moment I had walked into the past and my heart clenched in fear.

I read books about this happening. Of course, there was always a romantic interest to be found in the past. Things like that couldn't really happen, though. I'd been the one poking holes in time travel romances for years. This was insane.

I froze in place trying to take in what was going on.

I was too shocked to fully feel the fear that waited in the corners of my mind like a shadow. There was anxiety there, too. How to get back? What to do?

Then something hit me in the back and I stumbled forward, glancing at the floor. The coolness left and the room brightened.

"I'm sorry," Maggie said. "I didn't see you there. I'll have to watch where I'm going more closely."

I've honestly never been more thrilled to have been run into. I let Maggie pass me, and I walked into the dining hall that now looked normal. As usual there were corners that were in shadow, but I smelled what I considered modern food. Some sort of minestrone soup, I thought, and more importantly, coffee. That smell had been missing from the hall of the past.

I nodded at two construction workers who were eating lunch and chatting. Although I could have heard every word they said, nothing registered with me. I was lost in my world, busy thinking. I wasn't changing times because otherwise Maggie wouldn't have run into me. But I was seeing something from a time that wasn't the present, clearly.

I didn't think ghosts could do that, but perhaps instead of being haunted by ghosts I was being haunted by the whole darn Manor? It would explain all the weirdness that everyone talked about, like getting lost. What if I had walked around in my vision and maybe the kitchen wasn't laid exactly as it was and I wandered into a room that didn't connect to the kitchen any longer? Suddenly I'd be lost.

That didn't completely make sense, because then I'd have to have gone through time for at least a moment or I'd have run into a wall. I pushed that thought away. None of this made sense, not really.

I looked down at the food. I wasn't very hungry any longer, but I picked up a bagel that sat there and decided to toast it before slathering it with cream cheese. It would keep me going for the afternoon.

I didn't even get coffee. I went into the kitchen and grabbed a Pepsi from the refrigerator, nodding at Pat.

"Do you have any extra boxes around here?" I asked.

"What size?" Pat asked. Bob stood up from where he was checking something in the oven. I smelled something warm and savory but it was too faint for me to pick out yet. I wondered what he was roasting for dinner.

"Not real big, I don't think," I said. I shaped my hands into a smallish box size. Pat left the kitchen and came back with a box almost exactly the dimensions I had measured. It looked a bit smaller than I hoped but it was close enough. I probably wouldn't be finding a ton of flowers or anything.

"Thank you," I said, taking it and my Pepsi back out to the dining hall.

Nathan had come in but the others weren't around just yet.

"Afternoon," I said, sitting down beside him. My bagel was waiting at the table, getting cold.

"I wondered where you'd gone off to," Nathan said.

"Just the kitchen." I smiled.

He raised an eyebrow at the box.

"I found a pressed flower in one of the books," I said. "I saved it and figured if I find other mementos like that I'll box them up in one place. Do you think I should mark which books they came from if I do that?"

Nathan frowned. He ate a bit of soup, clearly thinking about it. "I can't imagine it would be that important. I'm not sure saving them is that important, although Bethany might like seeing all the things her family had pressed back in the day."

I nodded. "They might be interesting to be put under glass or something, particularly for the artists at the retreat. Who knows what they'd find interesting."

"Who indeed?" Nathan said.

Jonathan came in just then and grabbed some food, practically dropping things randomly on his plate.

"I am having so much fun. You would not believe all the pictures that are up in the nursery. It's like everything they took down from the walls they put in there. I'm finding some paintings that I really like, although there are others that aren't in good shape, but I think they're valuable enough to work on restoration. This is like a treasure hunt!"

"I haven't seen you this happy and excited since you began," Nathan observed.

Jonathan shrugged.

To me, Jonathan had always seemed happy and upbeat, although he was more excited today than other days.

"I love it when I start a new room," Jonathan said. "You never know. I'm so flightly that I get bored as I get near the end because there aren't any more surprises. And the last room had a lot of photos which I had to go through."

"You're valuing the old photos, too?" I asked.

"I have to go through the framed ones," Jonathan said, "because if I don't, I might miss a small sketch or painting. I have found a couple of etchings buried in amongst things like that."

"That would be exciting to find treasures like that. I just found a pressed flower," I said.

"Yeah, well at least you aren't hearing something whisper your name when you're working alone," Jonathan said, shivering dramatically.

I raised an eyebrow.

"And no, I don't believe in ghosts. But I do believe in mold, especially after the mess I found up there in the room next door. I'm surprised the whole house hasn't been taken down with it."

"Jimmy checked it out," Nathan said. "Looked like one of the windows was leaking for years and that whole wall will probably have to be redone, at least on the inside. The masonry will have to be cleaned, too. Heaven only knows how long that will take."

"I hope I don't find anything like that in the library, although I've been lucky. There's only one shelf that might have had mold on it."

Nathan started asking me questions about the shelf and the book. I was pleased that he seemed so concerned about the mold. It meant he was taking the care of the books seriously. Of course, who knew, perhaps he got paid a percentage of everything Bethany sold while he was working with her on valuing her collections.

CHAPTER 17

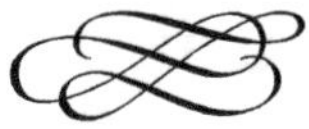

After lunch, I made it back to the library with no issues. I stayed in this time frame seeing only the real world, smelling the dust and mold, and listening to the creaks and groans of the house. When I had had my other-when vision I didn't remember hearing the house creak and groan. I had heard only voices.

Maybe the Manor itself was trying to send a message with all its creaks and groans.

The question was, what did it have to say?

I realized I was probably being silly with those ideas. The equanimity I felt about the ghosts and visions surprised me. For some reason I didn't feel in any real danger, though I didn't understand why. Perhaps it was a sort of shock, of not being able to take in what was actually happening. In all honestly, I was more concerned about my cell phone having gone missing, which, when I thought about it, made absolutely no sense at all.

Back at my desk, I settled into work at the computer. I entered the information on the books into the database I had and did a little research on some of the nicer volumes. This kind of work kept me busy and my mind occupied with mundane tasks. The books on the desk offered nothing unusual, not even a pressed flower or forgotten half-written letter for my box.

It looked like a beautiful day, and I recalled talking to Nathan about the walking path yesterday, but I'd gotten so busy I hadn't gone for a walk. This afternoon I'd done quite well in terms of getting more done. After the ancient history books I'd gotten to the Medieval and Renaissance periods of Europe and then a few books on Asia before moving into the Victorian era, which was probably modern by the library standards of the era.

Still, cataloging went more quickly when I was looking through books on the same subject. A few books had some damage, ripped pages, and one even looked like it had been nibbled on by a mouse, which considering the others were in pristine condition, surprised me. Perhaps that one had come from another home before finding its way to Schilling Manor.

I stood up and turned off the computer, still thinking about that nibbled book. I made sure I had my walkie-talkie and left the library. I paused by the shining white front doors, wondering if I could exit through them. I decided I didn't want to take any chances. I didn't want to get lost in a vision of another time, so instead took a route I knew—the corridor to the dining hall and then the kitchen and finally the side door. It was probably silly considering my vision had happened on exactly that route to the dining room, but this time I made it without mishap.

The fresh air felt good, and I breathed deeply. It had been too long since I'd spent any time outside. The smell of the sea and the grass was a wonderful contrast to the dusty old house. I would have to be sure to come out and breathe in some fresh air every day. My lungs were singing.

I walked across the parking area, noting that the cars looked pretty much the same as the ones there upon my arrival. There were a few new ones and I noted tracks on the grass where other cars had come and gone, probably the people working construction. I heard a power saw going in the distance.

As I got further from the manor, the saw became a faint white noise as it turned on and off. Now and then I heard the purr of a car driving on the road that was just over the hill. The path wound around the empty hillside, leaving me a good view of the Manor.

In the bright afternoon sunlight, the place looked like a broken thing. The front needed paint and even the shiny white front doors I had noticed the first day looked like nothing so much as a bandage, which, in a way, they were. The bricks looked worn with age and the mortar was crumbled here and there. The plastic on the roof was still waiting to be covered with shingles or tile.

The widow's walk looked rather unsafe, with the railing seeming to move in the slight breeze that came up. Above the house, a hawk glided on the winds.

I felt very alone with the place, thinking how perfect a photo of the place would be for a Halloween picture, when two workmen walked into my line of view. They were clearly working on the backside of the roof but had stepped up to the top line of the angled roof and were looking away from me. The contrast of their modern cream overalls and the ancient building was startling.

No longer a dilapidated old thing, it became a Manor filled with possibilities in my mind.

When I turned to follow the path once more, I was smiling. This was exactly what I needed. Perhaps Jonathan was right about toxic mold spores driving us all crazy.

I didn't hurry my pace, letting myself draw in

deep fresh breaths. It felt so good to be outside for a change. The sun was warmer on my shoulders than I had expected and there was a definite noticeable level of humidity, even for this Southerner. However, the breeze off the sea kept me from feeling weighted down by it.

It was not what I had expected from Cape Breton. I guess I thought I'd find a foot of snow in the middle of summer or something. This was like a vacation, exactly the vacation I had needed. I was going to have to thank Tessie, if I ever got ahold of her. I should have brought my phone. On the other hand, perhaps I needed this moment to myself.

I made my way to the top of the hill. The path twisted back upon itself, avoiding the few standing bare trees. I saw places where trees had lined this part of the path, which meant that years ago when those trees were in full foliage, it might have been a pretty walk. I even wondered, as I kicked a few bits of gravel, if there had been a planned garden on the hillside.

Finally, I reached the top and looked down over the sea. It was lovely with the breeze blowing my hair away from my face. There were low waves lapping at the shore below, though I could barely see them from my vantage point. It was pleasant enough to hear though. I loved that sound. Perhaps I should open the window in my room. I might be close enough to hear the waves, though the hill itself could act as a sound barrier.

Now and then, a car passed by on the road below me. It didn't interrupt my reverie. I turned to go back to the house when I became tired of standing. I had probably resembled a phantom woman thinking of jumping. Bethany needed to add a bench, perhaps a table. Artists would certainly want places to leave their supplies.

Turning, I saw a young woman standing behind me, dressed in pedal pushers and saddle shoes. Her hair was short and curled, probably with pin curls given the rest of her dress.

"Don't leave me," she said.

"Me?" I asked.

She nodded.

I looked around but there was no one else there.

"I am talking to you," she said. "I need you. There's so much that's gone wrong. So much forgotten that needs to be righted."

"How can I help?" I asked.

The girl turned behind her, like she'd heard something that scared her. I heard it too, someone walking up the path. I didn't see anyone. The girl disappeared. She didn't fade away. Just one minute she was there and one minute gone.

As I tried to process what had happened—too quickly, I realized, for me to even be frightened—

the freezing cold came up. I was shivering in the air that had felt too warm only a few minutes ago. I saw nothing but I felt every hair on my arms trying to stand up. All my instincts told me to run, but there was nowhere to run, except down the path, towards whatever was coming.

I stepped off the path walking directly towards the house. At one time I would have been trampling well-placed plants if indeed this had indeed been a garden. The hill was steep but not an impossible walk. Kids would love sledding the hill in the winter.

I remained cold for some time, but the footsteps upon gravel disappeared. I kept walking quickly. When I cross the path again, I headed down hill, walking far faster going down than going up.

Clearly there wcrc multiple ghosts in the house. One, probably Audra, who had an interest in making the secrets known and another that could be working at cross purposes.

Was the bankbook the big secret or were there more? What about the letters that were likely written between Audra and Eddie Hanna?

Was I really at risk from the spirits that followed the chill air or was I just being silly? After all, someone had taken my phone. If there was a thief in the house, were they dangerous? There were too many things for my mind to take in, to process the potential dangers. I realized that my lack of fear may have said something about my level of overwhelm. Given that, how could I trust myself to know what I ought to fear and what I shouldn't?

CHAPTER 18

Once back inside the Manor, nothing paranormal awaited me. The place was beginning to smell of Thanksgiving, or rather, roast turkey. It was only June in Canada so no one was celebrating a feast of giving thanks. But the bird smelled good.

The Manor was back to its usual creaks and groans as I headed up to my room. I wondered if either of the ghosts would follow. What if the invisible, cold ghost was trying to get rid of the girl? Hadn't there been a book with that sort of plot? Some evil wanted to eat the souls of the dead?

I know. I read too much. And I remembered just enough to scare the crap out of myself when I'd foolishly taken a job in a haunted Manor in the middle of nowhere while trying to forget my divorce. And to top it off, it was apparently true that I was sensitive to ghosts.

Could I forget my sabbatical if I returned home now?

Except, deep down, I knew I didn't want to. I wanted to know what Bethany had found out at the bank. I wanted to know what those letters meant. I wanted to know more about Audra. I became a librarian not just because I liked books, but because I liked knowing things. I loved the hunt for information and looking for secret clues. It's probably why I loved mystery novels and books that involved ghosts.

In my room, my lock stuck a little but I was able to push it open. Nothing was out of place but my laundry was gone, for which I was thankful. I needed my sweater.

I looked at my phone. Still only one bar. I took it to the window and stood there looking out. Three people were working on the greenhouse. The glass gleamed in the light. The modern look was a stark contrast to the ancient Manor. When things were done on this building, would it look as wonderful as the greenhouse?

I had two bars in the window so I called Tessie.

"I thought you didn't have phone service?"

"I'm in my room, standing by the window, and

I have two bars," I said. "Don't expect that reception will be great."

"What's it like?"

"I think the place is haunted," I said, bluntly.

Tessie laughed. "Is it two little twin girls like in *The Shining*?"

Tessie sounded far too happy that I might be in a place like the hotel in *The Shining* where guests were often murdered in certain rooms.

"Not two little girls."

"Then what?" Tessie asked.

"I saw a young woman, probably about fourteen or fifteen, dressed in those old pedal pushers and saddle shoes."

"Really?" Tessie said, her voice going up. "What was she doing?"

"I think she was running away from a ghost I couldn't see," I said. "I've also found a secret hiding place for a forgotten bankbook and a cubby full of old letters."

"You've barely been there a week! Can I come visit you? I want to see this place."

"I'm not sure about the rules on visitors. I know that eventually it'll be an artist's retreat so we can come up here then. Or not." Could non-artists go to an artist's retreat?

"I don't want to wait. The ghosts might leave before they finish all that work. This is too exciting."

"Someone did take my phone," I said. "But apparently it got returned. It's very weird. I'm not sure I like being here."

"Where else can you see ghosts on a regular basis?" Tessie demanded. "I think this is completely what you need. Something to take your mind off of Kyle."

She was right in that I hadn't thought of Kyle since I'd been there. To be fair, though, I hadn't much thought of him since I'd started packing up to take the job. It was like having a concrete plan had kept me from bemoaning my fate of having lost the man I was married to.

We chatted a bit more about the place. I talked about the computer program and the rooms filled with books.

"I'll probably have some sort of lung disease when I leave, it's so old and dank here," I said. "Plus the dust on the books."

"Do you wear your mask?" Tessie asked.

"I should live in it," I said. "But I really only use it when I'm cataloging. I'm not sure it helps though. It's so dusty here you can eat the air."

More laughter.

I wished I could enjoy the laughter and settle, but the brief moment in the sunshine was reminding me how odd this place was. How damp and dank and dark. If I stayed, would I ever find my way back to the lightness of laughter?

Over the top melodramatic. That's me.

"Hey, I hate to talk and run but I have to run," Tessie said. "Call me tomorrow if you can."

Which reminded me that tomorrow was Saturday. I wondered what people did on the weekends around the Manor. Did we all go to town as a group? Were meals still served? What about Pat and Bob?

I said my goodbyes with Tessie and then went to wash my hands and face. The water thunked and spit at me as I turned on the faucet and then stopped. I sighed. I wondered if the water was purposely turned off or if there was a problem with my bathroom. It was nearly time to go downstairs, so I decided I'd wait to report things until I got down there. Maggie should be around and she'd know what was happening.

I closed the door, locking it behind me, forgetting, for the first time, my walkie-talkie.

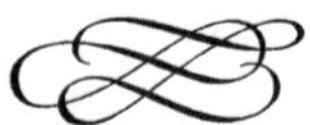

Pat and Bob were working quickly around the kitchen, which smelled heavenly. Roast turkey, stuffing, and potatoes, everything you think of around Thanksgiving, except, of course it wasn't November. No pie though. Not that I was terribly disappointed because I didn't want to overeat that much.

The familiar sounds of clanking pans and the clunk and thunk of the water system and the creaks of the floor boards greeted me in the dining hall. Clearly they had water even if I didn't.

This was the noisiest place I'd ever stayed in. I'd lived close to the airport in Columbia and that place had been quieter. Of course, there the noise had come from the airplanes, not the apartment itself.

Here, the outer noises were quiet but the inner ones were constantly rumbling and thundering like an unhappy stomach, which made me think of one of my favorite words. Borborygmus. The sound your stomach makes when it growls. Maybe the Manor was hungry? Now that was a scary thought.

No one else was in the dining hall but I settled myself in my seat. The sideboard near the front, where I served myself breakfast and lunch, was cleared off and tidy. The coffee urns were closed up and cleaned, the covers open to air out the inside, ready for the morning.

Soon enough Jonathan hurried in, looking over his shoulder.

"So someone else is here," he said. "So many people leave for the weekend."

"I was wondering about the weekends here," I said. I asked him about the food.

"Oh, they work all week. Pat and Bob are off next week. They work one week on and one week off, starting on Mondays, and then Janet and Tyler work the other days. You'll like them, too. Janet talks a lot," Jonathan said.

"And the cleaning people?" I asked.

Jonathan waved a hand. "Maggie is off but

she runs a tight ship. If there's a problem, she'll be available by cell phone."

Which would be great if I had her number. No doubt someone around here did and they could help me.

"How is your valuation coming?" I asked.

"I'm hoping to get an art restorer here in the next few weeks. I'm finding a number of paintings that I have questions about. There's work here that I just can't do on site, although I'm sure Rachel would tell us she could."

"I haven't seen her in days," I said, thinking back. I guess I had seen her at dinner last night but not this morning, nor at lunch.

"Consider yourself lucky," Jonathan said. "She's been everywhere. It's no wonder she doesn't finish anything because she flits from place to place. Now she's up near the old schoolroom where she found a room full of old furniture. I mean it all needs to be done, but I think Bethany was hoping to get Audra's quarters done."

I agreed. It seemed that it would go faster if Rachel were methodical.

"A lot of the antiques will just get sold. Bethany has talked about having some down in the main rooms for atmosphere, but the bedrooms will probably have a mix of the best pieces and then be filled in with modern items, like the IKEA dressers we all have," Jonathan said.

I nodded.

Bethany hurried in. "I can't believe what you found!" she said to me, not bothering to greet either of us. I saw Jonathan's face perk up. This was gossip he wanted to know.

"What did I find?" I asked.

"It's a fortune. It was in the name of my father's business, which has long since been dissolved, but because Robert Hanna died before the business was dissolved, all of this went to Aunt Audra but she never knew about it! As her heir, this goes to me as well. Not that I need the money, but it's a bit like finding buried treasure, don't you think?"

I made the appropriate noises as I took in what she was saying.

"The oddest thing is, is that while it was in the name of the business, no one else had known about it. It wasn't linked to any of Audra's father's other accounts," Bethany said. "It was just isolated on its own, which is probably why she didn't know about it."

"And the bankbook was hidden," I said, thinking about it.

"There are rumors, of course," Bethany went on, "that Hanna got Audra's father to help him run rum down to the states during prohibition. This could be where they kept those accounts. I wish I knew more about the Hanna family. I'd hate to take money that belonged to them."

"I could look into for you," I said. "While I specialized in preservation and archival work, I did go to library school and I'm no slouch at research." I didn't mention that research was my main love and if I'd had a choice, I'd have been a research librarian. It was only that those positions were coveted. Preservation and archival work was much less sexy, even by librarian standards.

"That would be fantastic," Bethany said. She immediately changed topics, at which Jonathan looked disappointed. Personally, I'd have loved to pick her brain a bit more about what she knew about her Aunt Audra and the family, but she had moved so smoothly into what everyone was doing for the weekend and then it was impossible to find a way to turn the conversation back to her family. It was almost like she didn't want us to know about her aunt.

Nathan came down while we were discussing weekend plans and he joined the conversation easily. Jonathan was going into Sydney for the day.

"I'll probably just end up at the library doing more research, but I can count on a better internet connection there," he said.

"I haven't been there yet, so I'd like to go in," I said. "I can do the research on the Hannas there, or a lot of it."

Bethany seemed pleased.

The turkey, stuffing, green bean casserole, and cucumber salad were all served at the same time. There were small plates of what was clearly homemade cranberry sauce, although it was limited in the amount.

Everything smelled heavenly.

Rachel came in about that time and seated herself. She didn't look pleased at the meal although the rest of us were all picking through things for our favorites. Maggie and Jimmy weren't around that evening. In fact, the lower part of the table was empty.

"Does everyone leave on Friday?" I asked, nodding towards the end of the table.

"Mostly," Nathan said. "I mean we have people covering, but most of the house workers leave and those who work on the weekends come Saturday morning. Those who are on week to week, like Pat and Bob, change over on Sunday night. So dinner on Sunday is always a cold cut assortment, rather like lunch but without the soup. If you want a hot meal, you have to go out."

"There's that tiny little place down the road," Jonathan said. "Mostly a bar for the locals but they make a wonderful pizza. Nice choice of beers, too."

At least going out didn't mean going all the way into Sydney, which was quite a number of miles. Of course, if I wanted something more than pizza I was clearly going to have to go there.

"What are you up to this weekend?" I asked Nathan.

"My work is never done," Nathan said. "I'm going to be looking into finding an art restorer that we can cut a deal with given the number of pictures Jonathan says need work. I've also got a few other household things that need to be taken care of. You might have noticed the water was off upstairs?"

I nodded.

"Maggie is finding a plumber, but I'll need to coordinate with them because she's not around this weekend."

I ate until I was stuffed. It felt like a Thanksgiving meal right down to the overeating. Perhaps it's impossible to eat roast turkey without stuffing oneself, a revenge of the bird, perhaps, for stuffing it.

I waddled up the stairs with the others. Even Rachel joined us.

"Anyone seen any ghosts lately?" she asked as we started up the stairs.

"Don't start, Rachel," Bethany said wearily.

"I think Lara has," Jonathan said. He had a wicked smile and I wondered what he was trying to stir up. I regretted having told him anything about feeling like I was seeing ghosts.

"It's probably just your toxic mold," I said.

"Bunch of rubbish," Rachel said. "The Manor is haunted and there are multiple spirits in each room. If you get scared, just call me. I'm good with ghosts."

I wasn't sure how to answer that and was glad my room was right there so I had an excuse not to respond. I entered, closing the door behind me. I wasted no time locking it.

I went to pull out my walkie-talkie from my pockets but it wasn't there. I remembered then that I had forgotten it earlier. I had left it sitting on the dresser, but it was gone.

I looked around the room and in the bathroom. I even looked under the bed, but the bright yellow thing wasn't anywhere.

I hugged myself when I finally gave up the search. I felt my eyes beginning to watcr, likc I was about to burst into tears, although I wasn't quite certain why.

I knew I hadn't taken the walkie-talkie with me. So where had it gone? And why did the missing walkie-talkie scare me more than ghosts? I could easily ask for another one when I saw Nathan, or even Maggie or Jimmy. It's not as if I was planning to spend my weekend exploring the Manor.

CHAPTER 20

The noises seemed louder that night. I heard someone running down the hallway. I hadn't yet determined what made that sound, other than a potential ghostly presence, but I did my best to ignore it. My best, unfortunately, was already thinking about the weekend and a nice normal stay in Sydney. Basically, I was doing a poor job of ignoring the sounds.

My toilet flushed by itself. I was sitting in bed, working on my computer, making the notes I had so been wanting to make earlier. I had set a new password to make it harder for anyone to break into my system, and I password protected this particular file. Perhaps I was being silly, but I didn't want anyone to know what I was about, not exactly.

My heart thumped a bit, trying to figure out if this was some weird plumbing thing or if I had the one ghost who needed to relieve itself. What an odd thing for a ghost to need, I thought. The toilet flushed again.

Then again. This didn't seem like something that would happen because of whatever had caused the water to stop working.

I would have called for someone but my walkie-talkie was missing.

Someone banged on my door, a loud banging that seemed designed to break the thing down. I jumped from the bed, startled, my heart hammering nearly as loudly as the banging had been.

"Who is it?" I called—if you can call squeaking like a little mouse a call.

No one answered. Not that I had expected them to.

The banging came again.

I walked slowly towards the door, my feet making the floorboards squeak beneath them. The Manor was playing with me. I was the mouse, it the cat. I felt certain of that.

I hid behind the door as I went to open it a crack and peek out. The hallway was dark. None of the lights were lit, an unusual thing. Normally they were lit all the time. I could see nothing in the darkness beyond the small circle of light that came from my door.

I thought I saw something move in the shadows. I wasn't sure what it was but I slammed the door closed. I heard something bang into the door, hard, like a cat leaping at its prey. I shuddered. Why did the Manor seem to pick up my thoughts?

I thought I saw something under the door, a flick of a shadow like the paw of a cat. I smelled the faintest hint of old meat.

If only I could talk to the place.

My bladder strained, all the fluids in my body suddenly dropping to that one space. The toilet flushed again.

How could I talk to the house? Did I just yell stop it? Would it listen? Would whoever had the room next door think I was crazy?

If I had to yell loudly, would Jonathan or Nathan, roughly across the hall, think I was insane?

I just wanted to find out what was going on.

The young woman in the pedal pushers appeared but this time she was in an old fashioned dressing gown with a tiny floral print. Her robe matched the gown beneath and there was only one button that held the robe closed at her neck.

"What would you say to me?" the girl asked.

If it was toxic mold, perhaps my insanity

would go away when I went to Sydney in the morning.

"I want to know why you're doing those things."

"What things?" The girl's voice sounded normal enough, although the words were inflected oddly, almost like a Scot might speak if he had never been to a city.

"Like the thing in the hallway?" I said. "What was that crashing into my door?"

"You were thinking about cats and mice," the girl said. "We picked it up and gave you a cat large enough for your mouse."

I was going to have rein in my imagination in this house. Or in the presence of toxic mold.

"How are you doing that?"

"I'm not sure," the girl said. "We pick up a lot of things from those who wander the halls, but your thoughts are strong. It's why I wanted to get your attention."

"You have it," I replied. I moved around her, feeling a chill but not the freezing cold.

The girl smiled. "What are you doing in the library?" She seemed very excited about what I might be doing there looking through the books.

"I'm making a list of all the books that are in there and then looking to see how they're valued." I wasn't sure what her level of understanding was. Just because she looked like a young teenager from about nineteen forty or so didn't mean she was.

"Why?"

"So that Bethany, who now owns the place, can make an informed decision about what to do with them," I said.

"Is that what the others are doing? The funny man who scares easily and keeps saying there's no such thing as ghosts and the weird woman who keeps telling us to go away?"

The word "us" was not lost on me. I wanted to ask who the "us" was but decided to let that pass for the moment.

"They're valuing other things, the artwork and the furniture," I explained.

"Why is valuing them so important?"

"When people inherit things they like to know what they have."

"They have what's here," the girl said.

"But what if they want to sell it? They want to get a good price."

"Like my father and his father did with the coal," the girl said, as if something had just clicked.

"Much like that, only the house and the things in it are the only things she has to sell," I said. "Are you Audra?"

"Among others," the girl said. "It is hard to make people see us so it was easier to make a pact.

We've been experimenting. So far, you're the only one who has seen us even when we work together."

"Who are you working with?"

"My father, his father, my grandmother, Angus the mason who died here, three servant girls, and Eddie."

"Hanna?"

Audra nodded.

"Were you and Eddie in love?"

Audra turned to listen to something.

"I have to go now, but I'll try and answer questions tomorrow. There are others that are thinking too loudly." She disappeared.

I hoped that my thoughts weren't so loud that they attracted the ghosts back to me. I just wanted to get on with research and note taking. Of course, after this visit, I wasn't sure how I'd settle in.

I didn't think I knew anything more than I had before, other than having more proof that I might be going crazy. But I felt okay meeting the ghosts in the Manor.

Audra's visit had left me with more questions than answers, although I was glad that so far my theories were panning out. This was, of course, assuming I wasn't just making everything up because of Jonathan's toxic mold.

CHAPTER 21

That night, I dreamed of walking through the corridors of Schilling Manor. I opened doors that all looked too large and too wide to be real doors. They kept opening onto yet another gloomy corridor. At first I was just curious, touring the Manor, but something changed.

I knew I was being watched, though I couldn't find who was watching me. I was looking around trying to find the person, only to realize that they were toying with me, like a cat with a mouse.

I began to run through the place, scurrying from room to room with a large cat behind me. I couldn't find a good place to hide and I was starting to tire. I knew of a bolt hole in a room down the hall but I had to get there.

I felt a stray breath against the back of my neck and I woke quickly, my heart thundering in my chest. The first pink rays of dawn were coming through the window, though it was early, far earlier than I had intended to get up. The room was in gray and pink shadow.

I heard the plumbing banging around in the pipes. Someone had likely gotten up and used their toilet. It was the sound the pipes always made. Too bad the construction crew couldn't have made quieter plumbing. What were the artists going to do?

I drew in a breath trying to calm myself from my dream. The dream had been far scarier to me than talking to the ghost the night before. I wasn't sure why. What was it that made dreams so frightening but the real unknown, presenting itself to your face, wasn't the horror you thought it would be?

The chemical lavender smell that permeated the room made my nose itch and I sneezed. The pipes had just quieted down and it sounded too loud in the room that was, for once, perhaps the first time, silent. Was I having a vision? But the room stayed the same and nothing jumped out at me. I pulled the sheets up over my head and tried to sleep again.

I tossed and turned and perhaps dozed a few times but every time I started to drop off, the house gave a particularly loud settling groan or the pipes decided to bang. Once, the radiator even decided to hiss and spit, as if it were still turned on. I was going to have to talk to Jimmy or Maggie about it when the weekend was over. If I decided to remain, I doubted it would be comfortable to have the thing on in the middle of summer.

I finally got up and went down to find that Pat and Bob were already in the kitchen. It was sausage this morning, if my nose was correct. They had oatmeal to go with it and the regular assortment of cold items. I got my coffee and my breakfast and settled in at the same place I always sat.

This morning I was alone. I was still alone when I finished my coffee. I considered going in and talking to Pat and Bob but decided against it. I went upstairs, fished out my purse, grabbed my phone and went back down to head into Sydney.

As I left the property behind I felt my shoulder tension ease. I breathed more deeply, despite the fact that my car continued to smell of old French fries. I opened the windows, letting in the breeze and the smell of the sea. The radio competed with the swoosh of cars traveling along the highway as I got closer to Sydney.

But the sounds were normal. They were traffic sounds, rhythmic and comforting.

When I finally reached the town, I was enchanted with the place. The homes were small and quaint, painted in a multitude of colors. I drove around for a few minutes just looking. I drove by the Port, without really knowing what it was as there were no ships at dock until I noticed the large fiddle.

I found a place to park, rather easily, as it was still early, and I walked down to the waterfront to look at the fiddle more closely. The air was crisp but not cold. There was a slight breeze that was a tiny bit chill, but the sun was bright which helped keep me warm. After looking at the fiddle, largely so I could say I'd seen it, I walked down the walkway looking out at the water, listening to the call of the gulls and generally feeling relaxed.

If someone had asked me what I expected of my work, I would have said days like this, where I could walk along the shore and breathe deeply of fresh air. I turned back and started walking up the hillside that ran down towards the port. It wasn't a steep climb and there were plenty of old buildings to look at. Most had railings on the upper floor and were graceful looking places.

I saw a sign outside one particularly old building that said it held tours but the posted opening time was half an hour away. I considered coming back if my research didn't take up the whole afternoon.

I found a Tim Hortons and decided that while in Canada, I would do as the Canadians, and went inside for a coffee. The smell alone made my mouth tingle with anticipation. While it wasn't crowded, there were a fair number of people, several of them obviously tourists with hats that talked about the Alexander Graham Bell House and T-shirts decorated with the words Peggy's Cove, a small hamlet down on the southern coast of Nova Scotia.

The conversation closest to me was about whether a sister would like it if they went back and got the lobster magnet or if something better might turn up that was equally cheap. Another woman was talking on her cell phone, telling someone she'd be by that afternoon with groceries. Everything was normal and ordinary and I was certain there were no ghosts. Not there.

I settled at a table and drank my coffee. It was too early to call Tessie on a Saturday so I just sat and enjoyed the street view. I enjoyed the fact that I wasn't listening for something out of the ordinary or waiting for the power to go out or wondering if I was going to walk into a vision of the past.

I was just there. In a Tim Hortons. Drinking coffee and listening to normal people talking.

By the time I had finished, I was almost resentful of the task I'd offered to do for Bethany while I was in town. I hoped I didn't run into Jonathan at the library if I went in and did research. While I would say I liked him, I didn't want to see him. I wanted to forget Schilling Manor.

In fact, if someone had asked me right then if I ever wanted to see the place again, I would have said no. But my job was there. While I had a full year of sabbatical, it wasn't like I was getting paid for the time off and I had to put food on the table. This job paid well. It would allow me to save up a tidy nest egg too, particularly since I didn't really need to purchase any of my own food.

I realized I felt trapped. It wasn't lost on me that my thoughts went to being trapped like a rat. Another image of a cat and rodent. I felt annoyed that anything about the house was ruining my escape to the "city."

I sighed and tossed my cup in the garbage as I headed out to the library. A woman smiled at me as I left. I wasn't sure but I thought she was one of the people working around the house, those mysterious cleaners that I might glimpse a little but not really see. They were more elusive than the ghosts, actually.

Which made me wonder if she really was a cleaner or if she was one of the ghosts. I'd hate it if they were following me and refusing to let me get away on my own. I waited a second to make sure the girl interacted with the young man at the counter. She did.

I hurried away from the Tim Hortons, feeling a little silly. And feeling a bit near tears that I was so obsessed with ghosts and hauntings. I really needed to get away from the Manor.

CHAPTER 22

The drive back to the Manor couldn't have been more different. My shoulders were tightening and I could feel them raising towards my ears as I drove. The sun was gone and the clouds were dark. When I opened the window to try and avoid the smell of French fries, which were no longer so wonderful, I smelled rain.

It was still muggy out, my clothes clinging to my body, although it wasn't warm enough for me to sweat. My body was giving off an odor that reminded me of vegetables rotting in the sun. Lovely. I would need to shower before going down to dinner.

I had spent the rest of the morning in the library, becoming more frustrated. I finally gave up and asked for help from a friendly librarian. She pointed me towards the historical society. I'd passed it on my walk earlier in the day. When I got there, they were open for another hour.

I went in and talked to a lovely woman who found me more information than I could have imagined. I spent the time taking as many notes as I could, purchasing a ridiculously expensive note-book emblazoned with their name in which to do so. I just couldn't type on my phone fast enough and I hadn't thought to bring my laptop. I had planned to use the library's computers.

I had some lunch and then wandered around the town, looking at various shops and feeling out of sorts. I hadn't liked the information I'd found and the implications of it. Sandy, the woman at the historical society was going to check a few things for me to verify. That had started the raising of my shoulders right there and no amount of retail therapy had helped.

The dark clouds that had begun floating in from the east didn't make the tension any better. I had given up and gone to my car, still parked down near the port, and driven back towards Schilling Manor, finding my mood darkening every bit as much as the sky.

There were only four cars in the parking area there this time. I expected two of them belonged to Pat and Bob. I wondered who the other two cars belonged to. I sighed. I'd purchased nothing but the food I'd eaten there and the notebook, forgetting everything I had hoped to look for when I'd gotten started researching the family.

I hoped Sandy got back to me quickly and that my phone actually worked when she did.

I also hoped that no one asked me anything about the visit until I was ready to share. I hate the idea of gossip, particularly gossip that isn't true, and I didn't want to engage in it. While I was fairly certain I had true information, I wanted to wait until I was certain before telling Bethany. I didn't want anyone to get fired. I also didn't want to have to leave because of hard feelings if it were all innocent.

Inside, the kitchen wasn't as bright as usual or maybe it was the absence of Pat and Bob. It wasn't dinner time yet, though, and it was a weekend. With so few people around, why would they be working very hard on a meal?

I heard thunder rumble in the sky as I started up the stairs. I was oddly glad to be back if the rain was going to start. I could have wished for more people around, though. The idea of being stuck in the house with only a few other people in a storm didn't thrill me. I hoped the others would return soon.

Fortunately, while the thunder rumbled its threats outside, the power barely flickered. I reached my room, pleased to see that not only was it made up, but that my laundry had been done and was lying neatly folded on the bed. I washed up and then put away my clothing, glad to have the sweater back as it held the walkie-talkie so much more tidily than my other shirt.

Not that I had the walkie-talkie. Of course, did I need one, really? I had a ghost to guide me, after all.

I pulled out my laptop and logged on, checking on my real life. I'd called Tessie after I'd left the historical society and we'd chatted about the job and her life and how things were going back home in Columbia. It was hot there today, unusually so for June, but Tessie never minded. She was out on her balcony in the shade having a sweet tea.

The idea had made my mouth water and I'd tried to find sweet tea in Sydney. I had spotted a McDonald's which does nice sweet tea in the states but they didn't have sweet tea in Canada, a huge disappointment when I was missing home.

It had added a small insult to other small injuries putting me out of sorts for the rest of the afternoon, just in case I hadn't already been out of sorts to begin with.

Now, home, such as it was, in my room, I took out the notebook and then got my laptop. I decided the best way to do things was to attempt to transcribe my notes and maybe reorganize what I knew.

Thunder crashed again, making me jump. The lights flickered and I waited for them to go out, but they stayed on. I made sure I had the electric lantern near the bed, just in case. I settled back in to do some work.

I was busy copying information about Bethany's family tree onto the computer when I heard someone walk down the hallway. It was an ordinary walk, not the thumping of the evening before. I smelled cinnamon, like someone was eating a cinnamon roll. My stomach growled faintly in response.

I considered getting up to see who it was, perhaps engage in conversation, but if it was Bethany there was too much I'd have to hold back, so I stayed where I was listening to the rain patter against the window and the thunder crack overhead.

Lights flickered every few seconds and my arm was tense from being ready to grab the electric lantern. The light from outside was becoming dimmer as the dark clouds rolled over what little light was left from the sun.

Evening was setting in.

I felt a chill creep over me and suddenly I didn't want to be in the room. I got up, taking my time putting the computer aside and plugging it back into the surge protector, which I noticed was off. I turned it back on.

I left my phone there, too, but grabbed the electric lantern and left the room. The chill followed me, like my own personal small cloud blocking out the warmth from the sun. It wasn't icy or freezing, yet I was in a spot that was just a little colder than I thought it should be. I almost sensed that the rest of the place was a tiny bit warmer than the space I occupied which was an unsettling feeling.

The lights went out as I was stepping onto the first floor. No warning. No flickers. Just light one minute and then nothing. The side door had a small pane of glass that let in a little light, leaving me in grayness. I turned on the electric lantern and continued into the kitchen.

Pat was swearing quietly. Bob was just frowning.

"Probably a cold meal," Pat said. I could tell she was mad.

"I wasn't down for dinner already," I said. It was at least another hour until six. "I just couldn't stand being in my room any longer."

"Be glad when this week is over," Pat said. "I'm used to the power being finicky here, but this is ridiculous. We've used the darned generator so many times that we're out of fuel. I called Jimmy so he can get someone out here with more, but that means we can't do any cooking unless the power decides to come back on."

I didn't hold out any more hope of that happening than Pat did.

"What had you planned?" I asked. Bob had pulled up a stool, waiting for Pat to make a decision.

"We do the big meal on Friday so that we just have leftovers out for Saturday. Then Sunday we do cold cuts. Makes less work for us as the week winds down," Pat said. "I hate to let all that stuff go to waste. I'm not here to warm it up on Sunday evening though. And I'm not staying, not after this week."

I had had no idea that they were having power issues in the kitchen and I said as much.

Bob shrugged. "We tell Maggie or Jimmy and they take care of it. No reason for the rest of you to know."

I nodded. "How long have you two been working here?" I asked.

"About six months now," Pat said. "Although I'm starting to wonder if the money is worth it. I live way down south of here, and it's quite a drive even once a week."

"I'm just over in Sydney but even that feels like a drive," Bob said. "I tried going home in the evenings but sometimes the weather is just so bad it's easier to stay here. And the hours are long enough, it's nice not to have to commute."

I nodded thinking about it.

"How long has Nathan worked for Bethany?" I asked.

Pat looked at Bob. "I think about the same amount of time as we have. It's you all that seem to keep turning over. Rachel is the third antiques person…"

"Second," Bob interrupted. "It's the art historians we've had three of now."

I nodded, not wanting to correct Bob, but I thought Pat was right.

"Course, after what the first girl art historian started telling folks who were local to the area, no one would come work here. It's why they have to hire people from outside of Canada for your jobs," Pat added. "Not that you aren't good or anything, but it's easier for a place like this to not have to hassle with work visas and things like that."

I nodded. That made sense. And the pay was extraordinary high for what I was doing, even on a temporary job.

"They didn't seem to have a lot of applicants even from the states," I said. "At least not for the library job."

Pat shook her head. "Lots of folks hear it's live-in and don't want to move to another place even for a year. Even if they do, it takes a special person to be out here in the middle of nowhere for that amount of time. I think they interviewed two other librarians before you. One was married and her husband didn't want to come here. He worked from home in IT but we have such poor coverage he didn't want to chance it. The other wasn't suitable at all, at least not from what I heard."

It sounded like Pat had heard a lot, I thought.

"Tell me about Jonathan," I said. "He's a funny guy and not the sort of person I'd expect to find out here."

Bob looked at Pat.

"Bankruptcy," Pat said. "He was so far in debt that he had to declare bankruptcy. I guess that so many employers check that now that he was having a hard time finding a position and he wasn't happy with the one he had. Didn't pay enough. I heard that he and Nathan talked about it and according to what I heard, this worked out well for him. He can't really shop while he's here and he can gain a good employment record. Hopefully by the time he's finished, the bankruptcy won't be the first thing a new employer sees any longer."

Interesting, I thought.

"And Rachel?" I asked.

Pat rolled her eyes. At that moment, the side door banged open.

"That's a heck of a storm coming in. I hope that everyone coming back gets here soon," Jimmy said coming in to the kitchen. "There's no way I'm going back out."

He nodded at me smiling.

"Did you get the fuel then?" Pat asked.

"I'll go out and get her set up," Jimmy said. "I'm hoping that we get a bit of a break before I do it, though. This is a nasty one."

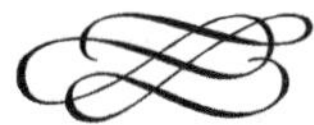

I waited with Pat and Bob while Jimmy went out to add some fuel to the generator. He came back in before long, once again wet, although not completely soaked.

I heard him in the hall near the side door talking to someone, probably on his cell, before he came back inside. He was so wet, I smelled rain when he walked by. Pat had seated herself on a stool that was partially pushed under a counter. I was still standing, thinking.

"We're in for it," Jimmy said. "The generator's been damaged and fuel just runs out of it. It's a good thing it was nearly out of fuel when it happened or there could have been a fire, not that I think it would have lasted long in this, but that's just what Bethany doesn't need."

"Well, I guess it's cold turkey sandwiches then," Pat sighed. "I'll get to slicing."

She stood up easily and Bob followed her. I wasn't sure how to help.

Jimmy went back out to the doorway and made another call. I wasn't sure who he was talking this time, but I heard his voice and it sounded urgent. He seemed to be keeping it lower than he had earlier and I wondered what this phone call was about.

He came back, his face as thundery as the storm outside.

"Is something wrong?" I asked.

Jimmy shook his head. "I think someone purposely damaged the generator. I'm not sure if they meant to hide the damage so we wouldn't ever notice and cause a fire or if they just wanted to be sure it wouldn't work. Bethany doesn't want me calling the police about it."

"Why not?" I asked. If there was vandalism, you'd think she'd want a record of it, at least.

"We've called them any number of times already for various types of vandalism. I think she doesn't want to keep on calling them," Jimmy said.

"Yes, but doesn't that sort of keep a record of the sorts of things that have been happening? And won't that help for an insurance claim?" I asked.

Jimmy sighed. "I'm not sure why she doesn't

want to keep calling them. There was kind of a pow-wow with her and I wasn't invited in, but when she came out, she was pretty upset. I don't know what was said but maybe they suggested that she was having this done for a big insurance claim."

"I can't imagine that they'd do that, would they?" I asked.

"They might not have," Jimmy said. "Bethany can take things personally even when you don't mean it to be. I know that some of the things I've said about her aunt have been taken badly, so we try not to mention the family to her. She gets really excited about certain things and really upset about others and you can't always tell which it will be."

I waited, looking interested.

"I told her her aunt had been courted by this guy down in Halifax, a historian of some sort who studied the history of Cape Breton. It was really a sort of romantic thing. I think Audra was charmed by him and they'd go out to lunch whenever he was here and he'd bring her flowers and chocolates, the whole romantic gift giving thing, you know?"

I nodded.

"He even brought her a necklace which she wore all the time," Jimmy continued. "We teased her about it. Audra laughed like she was a girl. I hadn't seen her that happy in a long time. I'm not sure what happened but his visits stopped in frequency and they sort of just drifted apart. I think I was more heartbroken than Audra was, really."

"What did Bethany object to?"

"The whole idea that her aunt had a boyfriend, as we called him, I guess," Jimmy said. He was frowning a little. "I never really understood."

I didn't either.

"The odd thing was that when I found out that Audra's father had been investigated for criminal negligence over a mining accident, Bethany was ecstatic about it. I hadn't even told her that he ultimately wasn't charged, although there is still some hard feelings around the local area about the Schillings. It's mostly died off, particularly because everyone pretty much liked Audra, what little we saw of her."

I frowned with Jimmy too, after hearing that. It didn't make sense. It was almost as if Bethany didn't want to hear anything that countered who she believed Audra to be. I wondered what sort of relationship the two of them had had.

"We might as well eat in here," Pat said when she'd made up some turkey sandwiches. She had a bunch of them on plates, ready for us to dig in.

I pulled up a stool and Jimmy grabbed one as well.

We all dug in, with Bob getting sodas from the refrigerator. "Unfortunately we can't make coffee," he said with a smile.

Rachel came in about that time, pausing to look at us almost in horror because we were eating around the kitchen counter.

"Pull up a stool and have a sandwich," Pat said. "No use spending time in that big old hall with just the electric lanterns."

"They're cold," Rachel said. She didn't smile.

"No power," Pat offered.

"Can't you fix that generator?" Rachel demanded of Jimmy.

"We need a new one," Jimmy said easily, eating. He didn't pause to discuss it with her, just taking another bite.

"What do you mean we need a new one? Isn't that your job to be sure you purchase things before they wear out?"

"This didn't wear out," Jimmy said. "Someone damaged it and it won't work right now."

Jimmy was keeping his cool quite nicely.

Rachel snorted and sighed. "I'm not sure how anyone expects me to get anything done around here. Just let Nathan get on me about being too slow and wondering what I'm doing up there after a night like this!" She threw up her arms in exclamation.

I didn't actually find the night that horrible. I liked talking with Pat and Bob and Jimmy.

"I suppose Nathan's in town again?" Rachel said. She said the word town like it was a bad thing.

No one answered.

"I asked you where the boss was." Rachel moved over to me and tapped my shoulder three times as if to make a point.

"I don't know. I'm not his keeper," I said, looking back at her.

"You didn't see him in town?" Rachel asked, stepping back, folding her arms across her chest.

Sydney was a fairly small town, but it wasn't like I could see the whole thing from any one vantage point.

"He wasn't in the library," I said. I avoided mentioning the historical society. I wasn't sure what Rachel would do with that information. She might already be aware of what I had found out, or perhaps not. I couldn't imagine that if she did know that she wouldn't have said something to the rest of us.

Rachel gave me a long humph and then glared at Pat and Bob.

"It's not a meat day," she snapped and left.

"Excuse me for not knowing what diet she's on today," Pat breathed as Rachel stomped out.

Jimmy just shook his head. "I'm surprised that

Nathan puts up with her. I mean someone else has to be available for the job, don't they?"

"I think Bethany is getting tired of all this," Pat said. "We all sort of want things done. The faster she can get the antiques valued and out of here or stored, the faster she can go through and do the updates that the central wing needs. That's when you'll get really decent electricity out here, too."

Bob nodded. "This is all so piecemeal. I'm surprised the place hasn't burned down."

Jimmy chuckled. "The basement's too damp and moldy, I guess."

I shuddered.

"I can take you down there," Jimmy offered grinning.

"No, thanks," I said. "There's enough damp and mold up here. And darkness. I wouldn't want to stumble on a body or something!"

"I can assure you, there are no bodies down there."

As if that was any reassurance at all. Certainly not when there were ghosts around.

CHAPTER 24

After dinner, there was nothing to do but go back up to the rooms. Jimmy, Pat, and Bob had rooms along the front side of the first floor, down a hallway that led around the dining hall, past a large room that looked like an office. Jimmy often didn't stay at the Manor, but he had a room he used when he did. Tonight was one of those nights. They left me as I went to climb the stairs.

"Call on the walkie-talkie if you have a problem!" Jimmy said.

"Except it's gone," I replied. "I forgot to mention it. I meant to."

Pat stopped in the hallway with Bob. Both of them looked at each other and then at me.

"When did that happen?" Jimmy asked.

"Just last night. I didn't know who to tell, particularly as it was the weekend."

"I'll be sure to scrounge up another one," Jimmy said. "They go missing an awful lot and we never seem to find them."

He sighed.

I went up the stairs that smelled of chemical lavender and dust. Before coming here I never thought dust had a smell, but now I knew that it did. It was a smell that tickled and dried your nose and made you want to go out into the rain for fresh air to moisten to your air passages.

I reached my room without incident and realized only then that no one had offered me an option of getting a hold of them if I needed help. Hopefully, for one night, I wasn't going need it.

I paused at my door, listening to the piano music. It had to be Rachel playing it, I thought.

I walked up the hallway to the door beyond mine, listening carefully. I thought I heard her humming but couldn't be certain.

I wondered about knocking on her door and talking to her but decided that was a foolish thing to do. I hurried back to my room. Inside Audra sat on my bed, her feet hanging off the mattress. She was back to her pedal pushers.

She looked up at me and nodded. "Did you find out what you needed to know?"

I closed the door behind me. I had no desire for shadowy cats to come pouncing on me.

"I'm verifying some things," I said.

"They're true, I think," Audra said.

"How?" I asked.

Audra shrugged.

"In the letters you pointed me towards, you and Eddie, it was Eddie wasn't it?"

Audra nodded.

"In those letters you talked about 'your place.' Where was that?"

"We used to meet in the orchard just beyond the old greenhouse. You'd think you could see through glass, but you can't, not really, which meant we could see shadows if we knew what to watch for. And Eddie had a reason to be out there. I would just be going for a walk if my father ever caught us."

A few things started turning over in my mind. They had met by the old greenhouse in an orchard, and now the orchard was gone. Were the frustrated ghosts, searching out their place, the reason the greenhouse kept falling down?

"I don't know," Audra said, reading my mind once again.

I looked over at her, surprised to get a response, and she laughed. Her laughter was high pitched and girlish. It made me want to join her, even if she was a ghost.

"Why don't I get cold around you any longer?" I asked.

"I don't know. I don't have all the answers. I think I could have them if I moved on, but I feel tied to this place."

"How well did you and Bethany know each other?"

Audra rolled her eyes, or did some ghostly simulation thereof. "Bethany is just my next of kin. My attorney recommended I leave the estate directly to her rather than her parents because she was younger. It would be easier to settle. I didn't really care. I hardly knew any of them."

"Bethany sometimes talks about you," I said.

"She and her parents visited when she was younger. I hadn't seen her in years when I died." It was odd hearing that kind of thing from the voice of a girl who seemed a decade or two younger than I was.

"I have to go," Audra said, standing up.

"Why?" I asked.

"I just do." She walked over to the door and went through it, disappearing as she did so.

It was an unsettling thing to see, I thought.

I decided to wash up after dinner and get comfortable for the evening. I could probably play on my laptop if it still had battery power. Or I could read on my kindle, thankfully charged. Instead I paced around, running through what I'd learned about the Schillings and the Hannas.

Audra's father had one brother, a younger brother who had moved to Halifax because the city was larger and there were more job opportunities. That was Bethany's direct ancestor. This had all been easily verified.

The Hannas were more difficult. When Eddie disappeared, he'd been a young man. He'd gone to war and so he had a small will which left everything to his mother. She, in turn, had left all her worldly goods to her two remaining children, Bryce and Tamara.

Bryce had died with no issue. His will had left everything to Tamara's children, his closest relatives.

Tamara had had a daughter very young, and that daughter had gone to school in the States. This child had a child there—I was getting confused as to how this child would be related to Eddie—and named her Rachel. Rachel had studied history and had gone on to get a job at an antique dealer's while she was in school. The rest, as they say was fate.

Or was planned.

The fact that I'd come up with a bankbook with the Hanna name meant that Rachel might be someone who was entitled to a part of that money. I didn't know for certain. I did know that

Bethany wanted to be certain that the Hanna heirs got their share if they were entitled to it.

It was why I wanted to verify that this woman, this Rachel, was the child that I thought she was. And why I had someone else doing that verification. I didn't want Rachel to know I was looking into it.

Someone banged on my door. At first, I thought it was the house playing with me. I willed it to stop but the banging continued. I opened it.

Rachel stood there, looking annoyed.

"It took you long enough," she said.

At first I thought she was reading my mind, like the ghosts seemed to. Then I realized she was only talking about the time it took me to answer the door.

"Sometimes I hear pounding," I said.

"Call me," she said quickly. "I can get rid of that for you."

I didn't quite know what to say to that. Anything I might have said would have sounded completely insane. I'd talked to the ghosts and they thought she was just silly sounded beyond insane.

"What did you need?" I asked.

"To talk," Rachel said, pushing past me into the room. "I want to hear all about the library downstairs."

"Now's not really a good time," I hedged. "I was getting ready for bed."

"Barely eight," Rachel argued. "Let's chat. Or don't you like me?"

Being a polite woman that I am, and having lived most of my life in the South, I couldn't exactly refuse her, not after a question like that.

Rachel made herself at home on my bed, curling her legs up under her, leaning back against the headboard. That left me at a disadvantage. I wasn't comfortable enough to settle in next to her. I moved my laptop and faced away from the doorway, looking towards her, my legs off the side. It wasn't that comfortable and I would have a crick in my back if things went on for any amount of time.

I disliked the perfume that she wore, a sort of floral thing that normally I wouldn't notice, but it clashed with the lavender scent in the room. I hoped that sitting near my pillows wouldn't cause the smell to linger there. I doubted I could stand it all night.

The house groaned once, but more quietly

than usual. If it was an assessment of Rachel, I had to admit I agreed with it.

"So tell me all about Sydney," Rachel said.

"Mostly spent it at the library. I wandered by the historical society and looked around there a bit and then went shopping. What I really wanted was a sweet tea, but they didn't have any, even at McDonald's," I said, whining about something innocuous.

"Sounds like a typical day in Sydney. Go and look for something and then you can't find it."

I smiled. I'd actually liked the city. It was smaller than I might prefer but it was pleasant enough. If it hadn't started to rain and if I hadn't been so upset that Rachel appeared to be related to the Hannas, I'd have been fine.

"What did you do today?" I asked.

Rachel shrugged. "Worked, mostly. That's all I do. I heard you found that compartment in the wall in the library. I bet that was fun."

"It was a surprise," I said, carefully. "I found an old bankbook I there and I gave it to Bethany," I said. I wasn't going to add that she was looking for heirs. I wish I could have asked Rachel what she knew.

"I heard it didn't belong to the Schilling family," Rachel pressed.

"It was in Robert Hanna's name but it had

Schilling Coal as well. I'm sure the bank has to sort out what that means. Was Hanna paid by Schilling Coal or was he a working for Schilling Coal and he was just the name on the bankbook or what?"

"No doubt Bethany will try and spin it in her favor. All these rich folks are interested in is furthering their monetary interests," Rachel griped.

I shrugged, wondering how much I should tell her. After all, Bethany was planning on trying to find a living heir for Robert Hanna. "You might underestimate her," I said carefully.

Rachel slapped her hands down. "Oh, for God's sake. Haven't you learned anything about the Schillings? They were horrible bosses. They were cited for unsafe working conditions and got away with it, probably because they were so rich. They dabbled in shipping alcohol to the United States, and when people died doing that in storms and what not, they said not a word, nor did they help the families."

"That's all pretty ancient history," I said. "I'm not sure you can hold Bethany to those standards. From what I understand, her side of the family was down in Halifax."

"Audra was just as bad. Eddie Hanna had a woman that loved him back in town but Audra was always acting as if she was swooning over him. He probably left to get away from her and live a real life. Not that anyone here cared. No one mentioned him again."

"What's this about? Audra and Eddie Hanna?" I asked, as if I didn't know.

"It was an open secret, if you knew how to do any research," Rachel snapped at me, as if she thought I was stupid.

She continued her rant. "Audra foreclosed on a bunch of cottages that her father had rented out. She wanted more space on the land to grow the Manor, even though she never married, never had children, pretty much knew that the place would die after she did. Even in her will, she's tied Bethany to it, not that I see *her* minding at all."

"What do you mean, 'tied'?" I asked.

Rachel shook her head. "Bethany loses it all if she doesn't keep the Manor up, even better than Audra did during her tenure as mistress of the house. Bethany was supposed to keep the orchards as they were, but all the trees were dying so they'll be replanted soon. It was too late in the year after the arborist determined that they weren't salvageable. If those don't get planted, she loses the place."

"What do you mean, loses it?" I asked.

"It goes to the Sydney Historical Society for preservation," Rachel snapped. "Like they'd do anything with it. But it seems typical of the rich, trying to force a certain lifestyle on someone else even after they died."

"I suppose," I said.

"So what did you learn at the Historical Society?" Rachel demanded.

"I was there so close to closing that I'm having someone call me," I said.

Rachel was leaning forward into my space. I scooted back towards the foot of the bed.

"There are treasures here, you know. I'm sure of it. Treasures to prove that Eddie Hanna had married Audra Schilling in a secret wedding. I've heard of a secret will, too. All this should belong to his family." It made me wonder about Rachel's mindset. First, she said Eddie had a woman who loved him in town and Audra's love was fake. Now, she said that they were secretly married. Which was it?

And, while she didn't say it, I rather heard the words "to me" in them. Rachel knew exactly who she was.

I stood up.

"I haven't heard anything about treasures," I said. "I'm just here to catalog books. Which takes a lot of mental effort. I'd really love to settle in for the evening and do a little reading."

Rachel glared at me. She shook herself a little as if she'd let herself go more than she expected.

Thunder crashed above us while rain hammered at the window.

To think I'd rather be alone in the house with the storm than be with Rachel.

"I suppose we all deal with the dullness of this place in our own ways. I really do want to know what you found in Sydney. Perhaps tomorrow at breakfast."

"Maybe," I said.

She walked out the door, passing me a little more closely than I'd like, but she left.

Once she was gone, I turned the key in the lock and leaned against the door. I had a chance to notice how quickly my heart was beating, how quickly I was breathing. I was definitely more frightened of her than I had been of the ghosts.

CHAPTER 26

Thunder kept me awake most of the night. I'd drop off only to hear a clap that shook the very stones of the Manor, along with my bed. I was glad I had the electric lantern sitting on the nightstand. At some point in the night the rest of the Manor lost power. I knew because I woke and felt someone standing in my room. I tried to turn on the lamp which wouldn't light.

My heart beat too quickly and my hands shook. I nearly knocked the lantern off the nightstand in my haste to find it.

I got the impression that someone was standing over me, even thought I smelled the faintest trace of cigarette smoke.

I fumbled with the lantern some more, looking

for the switch but not being able to press it. It was a nightmare.

It ended when the light finally came on.

I looked around but I was alone in the room.

As I breathed in, trying to calm myself, I wondered if there was another generator for this part of the building or if this section was just left in the dark when storms came up. It seemed to me as if artists would need light to work by.

At some point the storm calmed and the sky turned pinkish gray. By that time my nose ached from straining for the scent of cigarettes again. All I got was a lungful of Rachel's perfume and the lavender that permeated this wing.

The ghosts, at least, weren't playing games out in the hallway, for which I was grateful. For all that I might sit and talk with the young Audra, I still wasn't sure I liked the idea of actually seeing ghosts. Saying the words, even to myself, made my heart flutter, and not in a good way.

The gray was receding to pure pink when I finally rolled over and exhaustion claimed me. At least on a Sunday I could sleep all day if I wanted to.

I was awakened perhaps two hours later by someone banging on my door. I pulled a pillow over my head, not wanting to get up. The person at the door, likely Rachel, wasn't going away.

"Who is it?" I called out, still not getting out of bed.

"Aren't you ever going to get up?" It was indeed Rachel and she sounded far awake.

"No," I yelled back. "And I'd appreciate it if you'd let me go back to sleep."

"I don't want to eat alone in the dining hall," she called. "Please?"

I sighed. She was moving around out there, sort of stamping her feet.

I wanted to tell her to go away, leave me alone, and do whatever she wanted but just not with me, but another part of me, the part that had been raised to be a polite girl, was already swinging her legs over the edge of the bed and shuffling to the bathroom.

The part of me that spent much of my adult life in the South was worried that I hadn't let her in. I told that part to shut up. Rachel didn't deserve that much niceness.

I threw on my jeans and a long-sleeved shirt and took my key. I opened the door and Rachel almost fell inside, on top of me.

She righted herself from where she'd nearly fallen, clearly having been leaning against the door, kicking it from time to time, probably to make sure I really was getting up. She carried an electric lantern to light our way.

I closed and locked the door behind me.

Rachel hurried down the stairs first and I followed. Pat and Bob were in the kitchen.

"Just bagels, cold cereal, or fruit this morning," Pat said. "Jimmy has gone to see about getting the fuses fixed. He's been making calls all morning."

"Great," I said.

Rachel said nothing.

I took a soda from the fridge. It was cool but not cold.

Rachel sighed before grabbing one herself with the air of someone completely put out. She hurried into the dining room, already lit with the electric lanterns that were always at the ready down there.

"I can't see why they didn't have another generator to back up the first one."

"And if someone sabotaged it, then that would could have been sabotaged, too," I said.

Rachel shrugged.

We both had cold cereal with milk that was quickly becoming room temperature. I wondered how long the milk would last. Probably better for us to eat that up then than to have to toss it.

I was just finishing my Pepsi when Rachel spoke after leaving me to eat in silence.

"I need to show you something I found." She had been busy picking at her food and sighing. Now she stared at me intently.

There was something slightly off.

"What?" I asked.

"In the schoolroom. I was looking through those boxes of books. There's a lot of finds up there." She seemed very keen.

I wondered what she'd been doing looking through the books in the schoolroom but was rather afraid to ask. If Jonathan or Nathan had been there I would have said something. Heck, even if Jimmy had been sitting at the far end of the table I would have asked her. But not alone.

I felt the hairs on the back of my neck prickle.

"I'm sure," I said. "But I was hoping to go back for a walk now that it looks like it's clearing up."

Rachel shook her head. "No."

She stood up, coming around the end of the table, and pulled at my arm, like a three-year-old with her mother.

"What are you doing?" I demanded. She pulled me until my arm burned with her grip.

"I need to show you something," Rachel insisted.

I got up slowly, concerned about her. I didn't particularly want to go with her. No one else was around so far as I knew. Jimmy was down in the basement. If something happened, he wouldn't hear me, at least I didn't think he would.

Rachel grabbed the lantern and pulled me

along now that I was standing. I walked slowly, dragging my feet the entire time.

We exited the dining hall and entered the narrow corridor that led to the main entryway. The house settled around us.

The place felt empty. Even emptier than usual. It was as if even the ghosts had deserted me.

The gray light made the main entry look neglected and lost. I noticed a small door towards the back, nearly hidden by the ornate stairwell that was now open. It gaped like a dark maw. I realized that must be the stairs down to the basement. At least if Jimmy came up at the right time, he might hear me scream.

Rachel pulled me towards the stairs going upwards. I hurried to keep up, making sure I stayed to the side nearest the wall.

Stray thoughts about angling myself to push her over the edge of the rail flitted through my mind. I couldn't believe I was thinking thoughts like that even if I was thinking in terms of self-defense.

Rachel led me up the second flight of stairs to the third floor. She'd worked higher in the house than I had and this didn't feel familiar, although I remembered touring this part of the house with Nathan.

The floorboards creaked and groaned under our weight. This time, instead of thinking of ghosts, I was thinking of mundane cares like whether they would hold my weight at all. The ghosts and visions no longer seemed so ominous.

Rachel led me to the right and then into the schoolroom. The boxes were still there. The place seemed even more crowded with boxes than I'd thought before.

Rachel appeared familiar with the room, pushing aside two boxes to slide between them onto a sort of pathway through the room.

The windows that lined the room were tall. They had curtains on them which were of a dark fabric that hung crookedly, letting in some light. The day was still gray but at least it wasn't raining. My trained eyes searched for water damage around the windows. I couldn't remember if I'd done that the other day or not. I think I'd been more worried about rats up in the schoolroom, what with all the boxes.

Rachel was well ahead of me, moving through the narrow pathway, clearly intent upon something.

I could easily turn and run then. Perhaps back to the kitchen, to Pat and Bob. I couldn't imagine how that would look though. What if I was wrong and she didn't know anything about the bank-book? What if this was just Rachel being Rachel?

"Here," she said, pointing at a box.

I caught up with her and looked down into the

open box. It had sat open for years, the cardboard broken and worn, as if it had been opened and closed repeatedly and then left to rot. Several old leather journals sat there, tied with ribbons. They looked black, but that was discoloration, I knew.

"What are these?" I asked.

"Journals," Rachel said. "All of Old Man Schilling's journals. He wrote everything down. There are ledgers in the bottom as well. Two of them. One a sanitized version of the other. It shows all his criminal activity!"

Rachel was practically bounding.

I opened one of the journals carefully. The handwriting was cramped and decisive. Not at all like the letters I had read earlier. I could well believe that it was Schilling's journal. The page I scanned talked about his concerns that the mine wasn't producing as it had.

I looked a few other pages but nothing stood out.

"Fascinating," I said. I looked at Rachel again.

"Keep going," she insisted.

I raised an eyebrow.

Rachel grabbed the book and turned towards the back. Then she handed it to me. "There." Her finger landed on one line.

"Those lost in the mines included Hugh McLeod, Ryan Murray, Miles Fletcher, one of the Laird boys, can't recall which, and both Boyd boys. It was up to me to tell the families. Mrs. Boyd about fell into my arms in a faint."

I looked up at Rachel. "I read about the mine incident online."

"I bet," Rachel said.

"So?" I asked, wondering what she was getting at.

"Don't you see it?"

I shook my head.

"Nathan's last name is Murray. I bet he's related, and that he's here to destroy everything. It's why he's always on me to work harder."

I wanted to suggest that perhaps Rachel would get more done if she was actually working on her antiques and not searching through the books which were my purview. However, I wasn't sure she was stable enough to listen to me if I said something like that. I was reminded again of Jonathan's toxic mold thing. Maybe we were both crazy.

"I think Murray is a pretty common name," I said. It was in the U.S. It probably was in Nova Scotia, given how it was settled by the Scots.

Rachel shook her head. "I thought that's what you were checking at the historical society."

"No."

She sighed and then pushed past me, nearly throwing me over the boxes, and left the room.

Without the electric lantern it was pretty dark

in the room. The only light came from the places the curtains didn't quite cover.

I made my way slowly and carefully out of the room. The hallway wasn't lit but there were windows in the entry area that let in some light. I rested my hand against the wall, wondering about what Rachel had said. Was there any truth to it? Nathan had been strange about the bankbook.

I didn't really believe he was doing something wrong. It was easier to think that Jonathan was on to something about mold or chemicals in the house that had all of us going crazy. Maybe I needed to stay somewhere else, even if it cost me money. At least I'd be sane.

The walls felt gritty and dusty against the palm of my hand where I brushed it along, feeling my way in the dim light.

The floorboards squeaked in random places. I walked carefully along them, listening to their sounds, wondering if Rachel had really raced down to the first floor or if she was waiting for me here with other crazy ideas. Maybe she'd push me over the railing of the catwalk because I didn't believe her about Nathan.

Once again I reminded myself how crazy I sounded even to myself.

However, the only people I really trusted were the ghosts. Which said something about my slow descent into madness.

The bigger picture, I reminded myself. I felt insane because I couldn't see the whole picture. I mean, perhaps I was mad, induced by some sort of toxic mold or a chemical which I had laughed off, but even so, that left a larger picture that I couldn't see. I wasn't making things up about the bankbook.

I wasn't making up my missing phone or the missing walkie-talkie.

The journals might have answers. I'd need to read them. I wondered if Bethany knew about them.

Or Nathan.

I reached the stairwell and made my way carefully down. At least I could see the stairs through the pale gray light that came through the windows in the entrance area. Thank heavens for open entryways. I wouldn't complain about the waste of space any more.

When I reached the ground floor I paused. The hallway back to the dining hall was going to be dark. Really, really dark.

I could try and open the main front door and perhaps walk around to the side door. No doubt Pat and Bob would have an electric lantern that I could use.

I hurried towards the glistening white doors. Behind me something creaked. I was turning even before I had registered the noise.

Jimmy was shutting the door to the basement. He hit a light switch that blended in with the walls near the basement door. Lights came on in the entry area.

"Thank heavens," I said. "Rachel brought me up to the schoolroom and then she left with the electric lantern."

It was probably a trick of the light but Jimmy's eyes seemed to narrow slightly.

"What'd she want up there? You're the librarian."

I rolled my eyes. "She was going through the book boxes. She did find an interesting box of journals and ledgers. I'd love to sit down with them in my free time, so I'm hoping you can find someone bring the box down, just to the library. That way Bethany can get to them easier, too."

Jimmy nodded. "I'm not really on today, you know."

"It's no hurry."

"What else did Rachel say?" Jimmy asked.

"Crazy stuff, you know. Like trying to match the names of the deceased miners that were mentioned in the journal with people here. As if." I gave a laugh.

Jimmy wasn't laughing.

"What names?" He gave a hint of a smile, not the one he normally gave but one he might give if he didn't feel like smiling, which clearly he didn't.

"Just the last names of miners. Why is it so important?" I asked

Jimmy said nothing, almost glaring at me.

Then he grabbed my arm, harder than he should have. It hurt, probably more because that was same arm Rachel had grabbed. What was it with these people?

"Show me."

"Upstairs," I said, pointing.

"Come with me," Jimmy said, pushing me forward.

I had been worried about Rachel, a little afraid, but I was terrified with Jimmy. The change in personality was greater, for one thing. The other, more important thing was that he was clearly far stronger than she was.

I went up the steps, moving more slowly than I had but holding tight to the wooden railing on the wall.

"That railing is loose," Jimmy said, shaking it for me. "See?"

I looked back at him. He grinned.

The smile no longer looked friendly. It reminded me of the crocodile in Peter Pan.

"I see," I said, though I continued to hang on to it, even the safety of it was illusionary at best. If I screamed, would Rachel hear? If she heard, would she come? Better I should wish for Pat and Bob to hear me.

I paused for a moment on the second floor.

"She was worried about Nathan being related to the Murrays," I said, putting my foot on the step to the third floor.

Jimmy barked out a single laugh. "Murray's a friggin common name. What gave her that idea?"

I shrugged. "She wasn't making a lot of sense."

"Too bad," Jimmy said.

I continued up the stairs slowly. At least he was taking me to show him the journals. If he wanted to hurt me then, well, at least I had time to formulate a plan of how to avoid the worst of it. The problem as I saw it was that I had no plan.

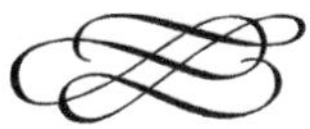

CHAPTER 27

The stairs felt shorter than they had before. My lungs were pumping harder than they should have, but I still wasn't getting enough air. Was this how it felt to hyperventilate? The way Jimmy was acting, I worried he'd let me fall down the stairs and then let my lie there until I died, gasping at my last breaths.

Considering the age of the house, considering all the leaks that were being plugged, the air felt surprisingly stale. A good flow of fresh air was what I needed to breathe fully. I was certain of it. But there wasn't anything. Just the weight of the dusty, unfiltered air that had probably been waiting a century for a pair of lungs to move it.

I tried to press all my weight down on the stairs to make more noise as I climbed. Was anyone who

I thought they were in this place? Was I the only one who hadn't had a prior connection to the Schillings? And why did no one like these people? There were plenty of horrible people who actually had friends. The Schillings apparently didn't.

I drew in a deeper breath when we reached the third floor landing, working hard to do it because my chest was stubbornly refusing to let my lungs expand. That led to more panic, which tightened my chest even further.

I'd never had a panic attack, although I'd read about them. As a librarian, I've been known to read a little of everything. I reminded myself that part of the panic was that I couldn't breathe and I needed to just keep breathing as steadily as I could. If I relaxed, I could breathe more deeply.

Being forcibly led into a hallway with a man who seemed angrier than he should, this was easier said than done. Relaxation did not appear to be in my future, at least not any time soon.

"Why are you doing this?" I wheezed.

"Don't be dense," Jimmy snapped. "Rachel told you, didn't she? That stuff about Murray was just a lie you made up on the spot."

"No," I said slowly.

Jimmy didn't even turn.

"Show me where that stuff is," he demanded, pushing me into the schoolroom.

He flipped on a light, which didn't help much. The lights were two overhead lights with bulbs that didn't appear to be much more than forty watts, if that. Clearly light in the schoolroom wasn't a priority, at least not now. There were places on the wall that I could see had once held sconces for light before electricity had come to Schilling Manor. I wondered how long ago that had been. Inane, I know.

I tried to breathe, pushing my way along the one path that led through the boxes to the one Rachel had found. It was still open when I got there, greeting me with the sight of leather-bound books.

I backed up so Jimmy could look through them. He pushed by me, a lantern in his hand, probably so he could see what was down in the basement. I was just glad he hadn't dragged me down there instead of to the schoolroom.

My imagination ran wild with what was likely down there.

The lights flickered.

Jimmy swore.

Several boxes crashed over right near us.

I jumped.

Jimmy wasn't far behind.

"Come here," young Audra said, gesturing to me to follow. She was between me and the door.

I hurried to catch up with her, trying not to wheeze too hard.

I was nearly to the door before Jimmy glanced over at me, a puzzled look on his face.

I was through the door then, with Audra. She didn't lead me to the stairs.

She led me down the hallway, towards the east wing.

"Where are we going?" I hissed.

"You'll see," she said.

She moved quickly, not bothered by floors that creaked or wood planks that weren't as even as they needed to be.

I followed.

Something banged into a wall.

I turned.

Jimmy came careening through the doorway.

He looked left first and then spotted me to the right.

I picked up my pace, difficult to do when it was nearly dark and I could hardly breathe.

If only I'd been further along, I'd have been invisible.

Audra paused, gesturing to me to go ahead of her.

I placed my hand on the wall again and hurried down the hallway, which switched slightly to the right and then a hard turn to the left. It was completely dark now and I had to slow down. Who knew what was down the hall?

I caught a whiff of roses and then one of spice. I hurried along, hearing Jimmy behind me, his footsteps echoing in the silence, the only sound but for my gasping breath.

Three steps further the silence was broken by music that seemed to rise from the floorboards.

Someone played the pianoforte. It wasn't the music I had heard earlier in my hallway. This was different. A waltz perhaps.

I heard voices murmuring, as if they were talking but they were far away from where I was. Still, I heard the sounds of talking and clinking glasses.

A woman's scream.

I saw a shadow come rushing out of a room, a chill following it. Another shadow with even colder sensation rushed by me.

Someone crying. The chill reached me even as I hurried away, hating that I was heading towards wherever they came from.

A woman cried harder, as if her life was over.

Something hit the wall.

A groan.

It was surreal.

I hurried by, wanting to help, but suspecting that whatever had happened had happened a long time ago.

It was lighter in the hallway now, gas lights burning along the corridor which seemed narrower than it should have been.

I didn't hear Jimmy, but I kept going and finally reached a stairwell off to one side. I headed down.

The third step down squeaked.

I heard heavy steps running in my direction.

I froze, half turned.

Jimmy was silhouetted against the gaslight.

He looked wild as he started down the stairs.

If there had been room, I would have stepped to the side to let him pass, but only one person could move down the stairs.

I ran down them, faster than I thought I could move. If someone had told me I'd take stairs in this place two at a time, going down, I'd have laughed, yet I was essentially leaping down them.

I missed my footing on the last one, sprawling into the second floor hallway.

It looked like the hallway always did.

Electric lights lit. No gas.

I thought I still heard the pianoforte.

Then the sound was gone.

Someone stepped on my hand.

A shadow ran down the hallway, past me.

I pulled myself up, watching the figure careen down the hallway as far as I could see, into the darkness where the electric lights didn't stay on.

I limped to my door.

Used my key to go inside.

I locked the door behind me, sliding down against the wood panel.

I was breathing hard but I was breathing.

Whimpering.

My ankle had already started to swell.

Audra returned to my bed. "I led him off," she said. "I'm sorry. I didn't think he'd get through the corridor so fast. We weren't strong enough to hold him."

"I made it, I think" I said.

"But you're hurt," Audra replied.

I shrugged.

"I liked Jimmy," she said. "He was a good worker, like his father before him. His father helped my father bury Eddie out back by the greenhouse, where we used to meet."

I was stunned. "Really?"

Audra shook her head. "My father caught us, setting up a fake meeting for each of us. He was there and accused Eddie of defiling me. There was quite an argument, with me trying to stop my father, but he wouldn't be stopped. Jimmy's father was there, too."

I waited as Audra drew a breath to continue a story that was no doubt quite painful for her.

"It seemed that Eddie would best my father when things got physical, but Jimmy's father hit

Eddie over the head. He was stunned. It was my father that killed him, taking a spade and slicing through his neck, nearly beheading him. I think I spent the rest of my life screaming. Not out loud, of course, but inside.

"The two of them buried him out there. I always kept flowers out there and visited," Audra said sadly. "My father tried to marry me off twice, but I always acted a bit off, just enough that the men were no longer interested."

She smiled, a very impish smile. It was surprising, given how she'd been rather formal the rest of the time.

I smiled back, despite the throb in my ankle.

"But Jimmy?" I asked.

"He and his family got paid monthly, whether there was work on not. A lot of money to keep things quiet. My father left Jimmy's father a nice bequest when he died. Jimmy expected the same, for his own silence about the tale. After all, look where it had gotten his father. I should have told him that I didn't care if the story came out. I should have told people before I died, but I didn't, and now look at him. He'll hurt people to get what he thinks should be his."

I sighed.

"Do you know who else is around?"

"The crazy woman who thinks she's banishing

us. The two cooks are getting ready to leave for the day."

I slid my back up against the door and limped over to my phone. I had no reception in that corner. I half hoped and half slid my way across the room to the window. I groaned a few times.

"He's coming back," Audra whispered to me.

I heard something in the hallway. The running feet like I'd heard in the night. Pounding against the boards too heavy to be real but this time I knew they were.

Then the thundering hammering on the door.

The knob twisted and turned.

A final thump against the door.

"The house can't fool me!" Jimmy called. "It wants me here. And you can't tell anyone what you found in that ledger. Not at all." He banged on the door again and then thundered down the hallway.

I wondered what was in the ledger. What did he know about it that it had set him off thinking he was being implicated in something?

I stood on my one good leg with my phone near the window. I called Nathan first. It rang through and I slumped in relief when I heard his voice, a real voice, not a canned response asking me to leave him a message.

I told him what I knew about Jimmy.

Then I called Bethany, thankful to have finally gotten her phone number.

Hopefully they could call the authorities. For now I was safe in my room, or at least a little bit safe. So long as he wasn't sure I was there.

I heard thumping and clattering around the house, like someone searching, loudly and noisily. I wondered what Pat and Bob thought.

I slid down again with my back to the window, watching the door, wishing for a weapon.

Then I heard another thump on the stairs. It was down towards the bottom but I knew that someone was climbing the stairs. It had to be Jimmy.

My heartbeat sped up. My hands got clammy. I began to breathe more shallowly.

My ankle throbbed in sympathy.

I pushed myself up.

Another thump on the steps. He was moving more slowly. Maybe he'd fallen too?

Audra had disappeared. I didn't know what more she could do. She was a ghost.

I pressed myself against the window. I looked down and saw that yes, it opened.

Another thump. Closer.

I flipped the latch and pushed it up. Thankfully, that was something that had been repaired.

The air was pleasant outside. There were

clouds gathering. I looked out. There was a tiny ledge of brick.

If my ankle wasn't harmed, I might make it through the window to stand on the ledge or to work my way down to the ground and run away.

There was no way I could do that now. I was librarian, not a ninja warrior.

I slid down to the floor and crawled as silently as I could to the bathroom, leaving the window open. I crawled into the tub and shower combo and closed the shower curtain around me.

All of that had taken three more thumps on the stairs.

My heart hammered.

The tub plaster was cold against my back and I felt a few stray drops of water, now cold, seeping into my shirt, making me shiver more.

Soon enough Jimmy was in the hallway.

Thump.

Thump.

Thump.

No hesitation but no running either. I wondered what had happened to him.

A bang on the door made me jump, but I huddled as far down into the tub as I could.

I should have hidden in the wardrobe.

It was too late now.

The wood on the door cracked.

Another squeal of pain from the door as more wood was torn from the hinges.

Jimmy thumped through the room.

I held my breath.

There was silence for a moment.

Even my heart stopped.

Jimmy thumped around the room and I drew in the smallest bit of air.

I tried to remain still but I knew I was shivering from fear and because of the chill porcelain at my back.

He slammed something on the floor. It was too heavy to be a foot.

I waited to hear the floor splinter but nothing happened.

Outside I heard a siren.

My shoulders relaxed a fraction. It was almost over.

At least I hoped.

Jimmy slowly thumped across the room, away from the bathroom.

I heard the floor squeak. I didn't hear the door close, but then he'd not opened the door, had he?

I stared at the white shower curtain, thankful that he hadn't come in here where he'd surely have seen me. I breathed in my own sweat, having to breathe through my mouth because I'd started crying.

Though my legs cramped and I was uncomfortable, I didn't move. I didn't want to take the chance that he was just outside, waiting.

The siren drew closer.

My chest felt tight. I needed air, couldn't figure out why, only to realize I hadn't taken another breath in too long.

I breathed in a little.

The shower curtain moved slightly.

I heard a thump near the door.

I imagined Jimmy turning, coming towards me with whatever heavy object he held, ready to destroy me.

Instead, there was only silence.

I waited longer.

The siren, now more than one, got closer.

Faintly, I heard something that might have been tires crunching on the gravel. Or maybe it was just my imagination.

I breathed again.

No sounds from the room.

My muscles were cramping, aching, demanding that I move.

I lay still.

Counted to thirty.

Listened for movement.

Someone banged on something far away, probably the side door.

I heard a squeak and groan.

A thump.

I tried to imagine what was going on but didn't dare move.

Something thumped across my bedroom.

Then the first thump into the bathroom.

A hand pulled back the shower curtain.

Jimmy stood there looking in on me.

He gasped, stepping back.

I pushed myself up, hardly leaping on him, but moving.

I screamed as loudly as I could.

Jimmy held onto a heavy sledge hammer. He was leaning on one leg, having fallen himself at one point.

He made as if to lift it.

I threw myself to the side, out into the bedroom, tripping over him, hurting my side again.

I screamed, "Upstairs! Upstairs!" again and again.

Thumps and groans from the Manor.

Jimmy righted himself.

Pulled up the hammer, trying to heft it as it to hurl it into my body.

"Stop right where you are!" a voice said.

The police had finally arrived.

CHAPTER 28

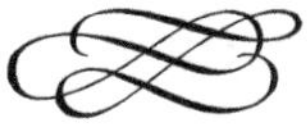

Nathan and Bethany hadn't been far behind the police, who took Jimmy into custody. Someone called for medical aid but I said I was fine. Which, I realized later, was probably foolish of me. Earlier, I'd have given anything to get out of the house, and now I was giving up the perfect opportunity to leave.

The police had given Pat and Bob quite a scare. They'd been out near their cars loading up to leave when the police had barreled down the drive, lights flashing and sirens screaming. They'd seen Jimmy earlier and then saw him going on a tear, as they said, but figured he'd been angry about the generator.

Rachel had been found down at the basement stairs. She was alive, though she wouldn't be coming back to work for a long time. She had multiple fractures.

When Jimmy approached her, Rachel had ranted at him saying I was trying to frame her for the thefts. She'd gone running to the library where he said I was. He persuaded her that I must have gone into the basement and then he'd pushed her down the stairs.

"I grabbed him, though," Rachel said. "And pulled him down on top of me."

Which was probably where he'd hurt his leg. It was too bad Rachel had been on the bottom of that pile up.

Nathan went up and pulled out the ledgers and journals, and he and Bethany and I sat around Bethany's sitting room. It was a pleasant little room a few doors down, easy enough to get to once I had a crutch, which, unsurprisingly, had been found amongst all of Audra's things.

Sometime during our chat Maggie had arrived and she joined us, wringing her hands and be-moaning what had happened.

Bethany's sitting room was brighter than most. The dark wood paneling had been removed and replaced with white carved squares of wood that went halfway up the wall and were topped by a white chair rail. Above that, the walls were painted bright yellow. Bethany had a large sofa and two love seats which were covered with thick tapestry fabric in cream with pink, blue, and yellow flowers on it. There was a low oval antique stool embroidered with a piano which sat in front of one of the love seats.

The floors were lighter wood than the rest of the place, although I think they'd just been stripped and refinished, as there was very little variance from the hallway wood floor, other than the color. There were pale sheer curtains which hung over modern mini-blinds, both in cream. Old-fashioned paintings of young girls with white cats hung on two walls. The third had a large painting of what looked like Schilling Manor in another era.

It was the most comfortable room in the Manor, I thought.

"Here it is," Bethany said, one of the ledgers open on her lap, her fingers marking a multitude of pages. "All the money given to Jimmy's family is here where it's just listed as services, except for one, which is listed as burial fees."

Nathan nodded.

"I bet that was for when he buried Eddie Hanna."

"We do need to find out if he's there," Maggie said. "The poor man shouldn't stay in an un-marked grave.

"What about Rachel?" I asked. I'd filled her in on Rachel's relationship to the Hannas.

"She knows about her relationship to that side of the family. It's how she sold herself on this job. While I didn't have many librarians applying, I had a lot of antiques dealers willing to spend time here. Probably in hopes that they'd not only have a job, but could increase their inventory," Nathan said. "No one knew she might be owed money. With any luck, she'll take whatever part of the bankbook inheritance might be owed her and leave so I can get someone we can all tolerate."

Bethany nodded through that. "I'll definitely make sure she gets something. As far as the other, what Rachel found, Murray is a common name around here."

Nathan shrugged. "So far as I know my ancestors were in Scotland and then the U.S. I have family in British Columbia but no one in Nova Scotia. If we're related it goes back way before any of this started."

So that was that.

"I found Audra's letters to Eddie and his to her," I said. "They're in the nightstand drawer under a few other things. Things kept going missing and I didn't want someone to take those." I refrained from saying how I had found them or telling them what Audra had told me.

"I'd love to see those!" Bethany leaped up as she spoke to go running into my room and find those letters.

"The police have gone through Jimmy's room," Maggie said as Bethany left. "He had a few old walkie-talkies. I bet he was the one who took things."

"But why the phones?" Nathan asked

"The police asked me to examine mine," I said. "They think he might have been using them so he could listen in on conversations. There was some equipment in his room that suggested that's what was going on. They also said it might be why we had such slow internet connections. He'd tap into things from time to time."

"And of course," Maggie said, "he was probably behind some of the house problems so that he could make sure he always had to be here."

I kept quiet about some of the things I was pretty sure Jimmy wasn't a part of. No sense talking about the ghosts now.

"So," Nathan said awkwardly, "will I have to find another librarian to work here or are you up for staying on? It's not like you'll be expected to work that hard while you're laid up. I bet I can get someone temporarily from the town to come in and help you move books so you can sit and do the data entry."

"I think I'd like that," I said.

I realized that I would. In fact, I kind of wanted to see Audra again. After she'd slowed Jimmy down enough that I could get away, I felt like we were friends. She'd spent time with me at my worst. I didn't want to lose her.

Bethany bounced back in with the letters. "I wish I had known about these sooner."

"If Eddie is buried out by the greenhouse, then perhaps he can be moved and he and Audra can be buried side by side," Maggie suggested.

"Oh, that would be perfect! So romantic, in a sad way, don't you think?" Bethany said.

There was a pause while we reflected on that.

I heard someone walk down the hall, light-footed and quick. There was a pause and then someone hurried down towards the sitting room, where the door was open for a change, the light streaming out in to the hallway.

"What did you do?" Jonathan asked looking at me. "Did something come for you?"

"It's a long story," I said.

"Well, you'd better start filling me in because I'm not going anywhere." He sat on the sofa next to Bethany and waited for me to begin.

I didn't hesitate to tell him all.

Jonathan's eyes got bigger and wider during the whole tale. At the end of it, he said, "I can't believe I was in Sydney the whole time, glad to be away from the Manor! If I'd been here, at least you wouldn't have been alone."

"Rachel was here," I said. "I mean, she was a bit odd, but she wasn't dangerous."

"Like that helped anyone," Jonathan said. And then he sighed. "Not that I'd have been any more help. I'd probably have fainted dead away, leaving you just as alone as you were. But I'd get to play a bigger role in the story. I mean if they made a movie, I'd get some second rate actor playing me now. It's not like I have a very big part."

Bethany laughed and got up and hugged him. "You play a very big part for those of us here. Who else could make us laugh on a night like this?"

I smiled a Jonathan and nodded.

Which he took in as his due.

I leaned back on the love seat and felt relaxed for the first time since coming to the Manor. I realized I was looking forward to getting back to work here, and for the first time since I'd arrived, I wasn't thinking about when the job would end.

ABOUT BONNIE ELIZABETH

Bonnie Elizabeth could never decide what to do, so she wrote stories about amazing things and sometimes she even finished them.

While rejection stung her so badly in person, she spent most of her young life talking to cats and dogs rather than people, she was unusually resilient when it came to rejections on her writing, racking up a good number of them.

Floating through a variety of jobs, including veterinary receptionist, cemetery administrator, and finally acupuncturist, she continued to write stories.

When the internet came along (yes she's old), she started blogging as her cat, because we all know cats don't notice rejection. Then she started publishing.

Bonnie writes in a variety of genres. Her popular Whisper series is contemporary fantasy and her Teenage Fairy Godmother series is written for teens. She had published in a number of anthologies and is working on expanding her writing repertoire.

She lives with her husband (who talks less than she does) and her three cats, who always talk back.

Stay in Touch

Little Dog Lost

Death Interrupted

Down in Whisper

A Haunting Whisper

A Haunting Attraction

Secrets Not Whispers

Only Human

OTHER NOVELS

One Bad Wish

Sun Spot Magic

Ghosts from the Past

Unnatural Secrets

Shadows of Solstice

Find them all at your favorite bookseller or check us out
at MyBigFatOrangeCat.com